WHERE'S MORNING GONE?

Barney Roberts was born in Flowerdale, Tasmania, in 1920. Apart from the period he spent in the A.I.F. and as a prisoner of war in Germany 1940-45, he has lived in Flowerdale all his life either as a farmer or in his Bush House as a writer. This is his sixth book. The others include two books of poetry, *The Phantom Boy* and *Stones in the Cephissus*, a novel, *The Penalty of Adam*, and his P.O.W. memoirs, *A Kind of Cattle*, for which he won the New South Wales Premier's Literary Award Special Award for the International Year of Peace in 1986.

Where's Morning Gone?

BARNEY·ROBERTS

McPHEE GRIBBLE/PENGUIN BOOKS

McPhee Gribble Publishers Pty Ltd
66 Cecil Street
Fitzroy, Victoria, 3065, Australia

Penguin Books Australia Ltd,
487 Maroondah Highway, P.O. Box 257
Ringwood, Victoria, 3134, Australia
Penguin Books Ltd,
Harmondsworth, Middlesex, England
Penguin Books,
40 West 23rd Street, New York, N.Y. 10010, U.S.A.
Penguin Books Canada Ltd,
2801 John Street, Markham, Ontario, Canada L3R 1B4
Penguin Books (N.Z.) Ltd,
182-190 Wairau Road, Auckland 10, New Zealand

First published by McPhee Gribble Publishers
in association with Penguin Books Australia 1987
Copyright © Barney Roberts, 1987

Typeset in Goudy by Bookset, Melbourne
Made and printed in Australia by
Australian Print Group

National Library of Australia
Cataloguing-in-Publication data

Roberts, Barney, 1920- .
Where's morning gone?
ISBN 0 14 010523 8
1. Roberts, Barney, 1920- – Biography. 2. Authors,
Australian – 20th century – Biography. I. Title.
A828'.309

Acknowledgement is made to the publications in which the following stories
first appeared: 'The Pea Game' in *Australian Short Stories* and 'The Skylark'
in *A Bundle of Yarns*, Michael Cavanagh (ed.), Oxford University Press,
Melbourne, 1986.

McPhee Gribble's creative writing programme is assisted by
the Literature Board of the Australia Council.

For Frank, Loch, Judith and Henry with love
(remembering their parents Knyvet Roberts and Amelia Hagan)

CONTENTS

To make my love more delicate
    I say into her eyes
The evening is the morning, dear,
    but in a sweet disguise.
The morning was too loud with light
    and the many birds would sing —
Who but the thoughtless would exchange
    the Autumn for the Spring.

Shaw Neilson, 'The Evening is the Morning'

Towards nightfall waking from the fearful
half sleep of a hot afternoon
at our first house, in Mitchelton,
I ran to find my mother, calling
for breakfast. Laughing, 'It will soon
be night, you goose,' her long hair falling
down to her waist, she dried my tearful
face as I sobbed, 'Where's morning gone?'

Gwen Harwood, 'The Violets'

AUTHOR'S NOTE

This is the story of a boy growing up with his sister, Judith, his brothers, Frank, Loch and Henry, under the loving guidance of their parents, on a farm in the Flowerdale valley in North West Tasmania in the nineteen twenties and thirties.

The names of several of the characters have been changed; a few others will not be recognized by those who shared with me some of these experiences. They are composite characters who nevertheless depict the life and times as I see them in retrospect.

My friends and siblings would interpret things differently. This is normal, for what is truth? – 'Pilate saith unto him, What is truth? And when he had said this, he went out again unto the Jews.' John 18:38

I thank Gwen Harwood for the poem from which I chose the title; John Shaw Neilson and also those many poets and authors who helped to 'grow me up'.

Barney Roberts

PERHAPS TOMORROW

It is eight o'clock in the evening on the 24th day of May 1928.

Bern is eight years three months and twenty-four days old.

He hates school.

His younger brother, Henry, is already sound asleep; his older sister and brother, Judith and Loch, are talking with their father in the diningroom. Frank, the oldest in the family, is fourteen and away at school in Launceston. Bern wonders if he hates school too.

His mother has just left his room. They had a long discussion about school and Rover and other things that worried him. She finished up by saying: 'Now just remember, you've got to listen to what people say, but the only one who can decide what's right or wrong is you.' She had blown out the candle, kissed him and left quietly after he had said he would sleep now. But he will not. Not yet. Things are too hard to understand. He didn't want to talk anymore. He wanted to think.

Bern hates school. That's the main trouble.

The day started well, then everything went wrong. There was a white frost and when he got up he put a saucer of milk on the lawn. It froze and he had iced milk on his porridge. His mother was happy. She and his younger brother were laughing about something when he walked into the kitchen.

1

She has a beautiful laugh and when he hears it, it makes him feel good. After breakfast he went to the cowshed to get a billy of milk. The sun was shining.

The cows that his father had milked were standing outside the shed with slack udders. The sun was prickling their bodies. They were chewing their cuds and looking at him with eyes that were big and round and speckled black. He passed close enough to stroke Roaney's belly. She shivered that part of her which he touched so that he laughed and stroked her again. She stood quietly blowing nostrils of steam.

Then he saw Rover. He is not much of a cattle dog, his father says, but the friendliest dog you could ever have. You only had to look at him and his tail would start moving; and if he was lying down, thumping. He had a way of smiling, baring his top teeth and snuffling; and a way of singing, sitting on his bottom with his nose reaching straight up when you played the mouthorgan.

There was Rover, lying on a bag, with cuts and gashes along his back and head split open. At first Bern thought the dog was dead, then he saw it was breathing. He stroked his side, but he didn't move. He rushed out to his father who told him Rover was seriously injured and might die. He told him he had evidently been caught in one of Mr Lynch's rabbit traps and that the man had probably thought he had killed him and had thrown him into the river. His father had found Rover lying in the paddock when he had gone to get the cows.

When they left for school their father and mother were both there dressing Rover's wounds. Their mother smiled and said she thought the dog might get better.

The paddocks were white and brittle with frost. You could see their tracks all the way from the house to the railway line, where whiskers of frost were stuck on the sleepers and the steel rails. The white gravel stones and the red dirt in the cuttings were lifted with glass pillars of frost and crunched under their feet. The water in Norton's sheepdip was frozen and the ice didn't break when they threw stones on it.

They joined up with a mob of Moorleah and Ballast Pit kids, where the railway line crossed the road. Some had pulled the sleeves of their jumpers down over their hands. Jessie, one of the big girls, was wearing a pair of old socks for gloves. She smiled at Bern. One of the big boys had rabbit skins around his feet in place of socks and his boots were tied up with binder twine because the soles were falling off. He had torn a hole in the seat of his pants climbing over a fence. 'You'll get a belting when you get home,' his brother said, as if it was something which happened often.

By the time they arrived at school the sky was clouded over. Bern felt sorry for Hong, his young brother, who had to sit on the closed-in verandah, with a monitor for a teacher. Because Bern was in third class he was in the big room with the others, twenty-one of them altogether, and Mrs Crammer let them light the fire.

Bern still couldn't do mental arithmetic and because he knew he would be kept in or get the cuts if he didn't get any right, he copied some of the answers others put down. Mrs Webster caught him cheating, as she called it, and gave him a cut with the cane and told him he would get another if he didn't get more than five right. He didn't get any right. He could only think of getting the cuts. She gave him two more for not trying.

Afterwards Mrs Webster told them a councillor was coming to talk to them about Empire Day. She said the British Empire was the greatest empire since the Roman Empire. Had anyone ever heard of the Roman Empire?

Bern put up his hand. 'The Roman Empire was founded by Romulus,' he said. 'Romulus and his twin brother Remus were suckled by a wolf, and brought up by a farmer and his wife. The twin's mother was killed by her uncle, the King, because she was not a virgin –'

'Stop!' said Mrs Webster. Where did he learn all that? His mother had told him. Some of the other children were tittering. The teacher told everyone to be quiet. They were not there to talk about the Roman but the British Empire.

When the councillor came Bern recognized Mr Schafbloken, a local farmer. They were all marched out to the playground by the big chestnut tree. Two of the big boys had to hoist the Union Jack up the flagpole, while they all stood to attention and saluted the flag, then they sang God Save the King.

Mr Schafbloken talked for a long time about our empire, and how a lot of people laid down their lives, and how only for Billy Hughes and Captain Cook and the Anzacs, they wouldn't be where they were today. He talked about God and Queen Victoria and the Great Bert Hinkler who flew all the way from the Mother Country in sixteen days. And he talked about all the countries on the map marked in red, and how someday nearly all the countries in the world would be coloured red. And to mark his word!

Then he pulled out a big bag of boiled lollies from his pocket and announced that there would now be a lolly scramble, because the Council wanted all the schoolchildren to remember Empire Day as a joyful occasion.

'Right!' he said, filling his big brown hand. 'When I count FREE!' His body and arm swung in unison to his counting. His face beamed in anticipation: 'One . . . Two . . . Free!'

The lollies soared into the air. 'Go oh!' he yelled. 'Git into it!'

Because Bern was small he was carried forward into the mêlée.

A second and a third handful must have followed the first, for Bern felt them dropping on him, and saw them, orange-pink with yellow stripes, landing on the red dirt and gravel around him.

Hands snatched at them. Someone's knee dug into his neck; a hob-nailed boot crunched on his hand. A few of the first and second class kids started to yell. Mrs Webster's whistle shrilled above the din. As if by magic the lines were restored. One solitary boiled lolly lay near the councillor's boot.

One little girl's ear was bleeding. A small boy was holding a rag to a bloody nose. He was leaning forward so that the blood dripped onto the dirt at his feet.

'They were a bit rough,' Mr Schafbloken said, with a smirk. Mrs Webster ignored him. 'Now, children,' she said, 'Say: thankyou, Mr Schafbloken!' They chorused obediently. She detailed two big girls to look after the injured ones, then turned to the others: 'Now back to your classrooms,' she ordered, 'and sit quietly with fingers locked until I come.'

Soon afterwards, they heard the councillor's horse canter off down the road and Mrs Webster burst back into the schoolroom. Her face was red like it always was when she was angry. She marched over to the piano, reached behind it for the cane and thumped it down onto the table. 'That was a disgraceful performance!' she shouted. 'Disgraceful!' And thumped the table again. She went on about good manners – 'If you couldn't have a lolly scramble without brutish behaviour . . . Well! A shocking exhibition! What would Mr Schafbloken have thought? It was a wonder someone was not seriously hurt.' Because they were all guilty except the little ones on the verandah, they would all stay in the lunch hour and write out in their best handwriting, ten times for third and fourth classes and twenty times for the remainder, this line: (and she wrote on the blackboard) I MUST ALWAYS BEHAVE PROPERLY.

Bern struggled with his lines. He tried not to think about what he was forced to write and pledged silently that someday he would be a teacher and treat children fairly and with understanding as they should be treated.

5

The afternoon session dragged. It seemed hours before the three o'clock bell and he was free to leave. He let his young brother walk on with a friend and followed slowly on his own, absently kicking at stones, occasionally standing to stare at the brown shafts of willow, or at the heaving clouds that almost seemed to rumble as they surged in from behind the hill, or to pelt a stone at a post.

Bern knew that Rover was dead. He knew without asking. Instead he asked, 'When did Rover die?'

'Just after dinnertime,' his mother said, 'I'm sorry'. And rested a hand on his shoulder. He cried a little then and drank his milk and ate his sandwich. 'Would you take a cauliflower over to Mr Gregg?' she said. 'He's digging potatoes at the back of the stable.'

Bern liked Mr Gregg. He was a melancholy man. Always he seemed to find something to growl about, but Bern always accepted his gloom, and so too did his mother who said she could understand anybody growling if they had as many children and as little money as Mr Gregg. Bern's father was impatient with the man. 'If he spent as much time in his garden as he did sitting on the rock at the corner of the house, he'd have the best garden in the district,' he said once. But his mother had replied that some people get to the stage when they can see no hope any more. She always grew enough vegetables to give some to the Greggs.

'You're a good lad,' Mr Gregg said. 'And your mother is a good woman. The likes of us can do with a bit of a help along every now and again. And how's school?'

'No good.'

'No good!'

'Terrible!'

Mr Gregg leaned on his fork handle. 'You mean to say that you don't like school?'

'I hate it.'

'Now you take my word, son, the schooldays are the best

days of your life. Look at your father and mother. Work! Look at me! Just one long grind, day after day, year-in, year-out. You make the best of it, boy!'

'Did you know old Rover died?' Bern said.

'Killed. Yes, I know. I saw him. That bloke Lynch wants a taste of his own medicine.'

Bern's depression continued and after tea when his mother went in to say goodnight she sat on the side of the bed and said: 'What's the matter, Bern? It's not just Rover, is it?'

'No.' She had a way of knowing. Bern thought he would never be able to hide anything from his mother.

'It's school, isn't it!'

'Yes.'

'Sometimes I hated school,' his mother said. 'And sometimes people too, for what they did.'

'You did?'

She nodded. 'But tell me, what went wrong?'

'I can't do mental arithmetic.'

'Why didn't you tell me before? We'll do some together, tomorrow.'

He told her about cheating and getting the cuts.

And what Mr Schafbloken had said about Empire Day.

And the lolly scramble.

And being kept in for what wasn't his fault.

And about Mr Gregg: Mr Gregg had said that schooldays were the best days of your life. (Bern's mother said that the best days of your life were today and tomorrow – if today is not the best, then tomorrow.)

And about Rover. How could anyone hit Rover like that with a trapping hoe?

And about Mr Gregg. Why does he have to be poor?

Long after his mother had gone, and he knew that everyone else had gone to bed, Bern lay listening to the night noises and wondering. It was good in bed, in his room, but there were sounds from outside that he knew nothing about, sounds of movement that frightened him; sounds of the dark. There was another world out there and someday he would have to learn about it. He knew he would learn about mental arithmetic. He knew that someday he would be one of the big kids. He knew that he would never get away from the Lynches and the Websters. And that always there would be the Greggs and the Schafblokens. And that the bigger kids would always tread on the littler ones – and Mr Gregg had said . . .

Bern turned on to his stomach and so that nobody would hear him he lay with his face jammed into his pillow.

THE ANNIVERSARY

To talk about the anniversary in Flowerdale would be to talk
about the annual Methodist celebrations, when most people
in the district turned up at the local church hall in their
Sunday clothes: most people, that is, except the C of Es and
the Romans, and the few families who claimed no God, and
the Bollings who didn't go to any church, and whom no
church wanted because they were no-gooders.

Mothers worked for weeks before anniversary day to make
new dresses for the girls and new shirts and trousers for the
boys. It was the gala day of the year.

The anniversaries we heard little about were the wedding
anniversaries. Sometimes Mum remembered but I think Dad
usually forgot, except once that I know of.

I remember that morning particularly. There was a cold
wind blowing sleet from the south west. Hong and I were in
the kitchen doing nothing, just waiting for breakfast. We
were quiet, as Mum was having trouble with the stove, poking and pushing at the wood that wouldn't seem to burn:
'This stupid wood!' It was the way she said it, that made us
keep quiet.

She had already pulled out the bit of angled sheet-iron
that Dad had fashioned and insisted on placing at the back of
the fire-box every night when he set the fire for next morning. He always placed it against the draught to stop, as he

said, all the heat from going up the chimney, because the damper didn't work properly. And as regularly as he put it in Mum would pull it out and stand it in the chimney corner at the rear of the hob. I don't think I ever heard either of them complaining to the other about the thing. Putting it in and taking it out was routine.

But today the wood was not good. It had come from an old dead white-gum which Dad and Bob had cut down in the creek at the top end of the Far Flat. We had heard complaints about the wood before but never so much as on this morning. And because the wind had blown the iron off the small wood and it was wet, and because I had forgotten to fill the wood-box, and because the fire wouldn't go and the breakfast wouldn't cook – the fat in the frying pan wasn't even sizzling – Mum turned on me: 'For goodness sake, go and get some wood that burns, and next time don't forget to fill the wood-box – this stupid wet wood – not you, Henry,' she said, as Hong was about to follow me out the door, 'and don't go without your hat and coat – and not your good school one – take a bag, there's one there on the nail – and you, Henry, get your boots and clean them –'

I took a bag, pressed one corner into the other and put it over my head and shoulders like a hood. I remember the time when Mum and Loch and Judy, with chaff-bags over their heads, and all of them laughing, came running up the path, with Mum a long last, after putting the calves out of the spuds in the mangold patch. But that was another day.

I knew where there was some dry wood in the tank shed at the dairy, wood Loch had cut especially for the dairy copper when he was home on holidays. I walked down the garden path, turning sideways so that my back was into the rain. I stood in the shelter of the dairy wall watching my father carrying a load of hay out to the cows.

It always surprised me that he could carry such a mountain on his back. Compared with most farmers he was small, but he had wide shoulders and was very strong.

I liked going with him to feed the cattle. The huge stack in the Four Acre, and the wide-bladed hay knife, kept sharp as a scythe blade, with its long handle stuck out at right angles, to slice down another section. The smell of it always brought back haytime, Christmas holidays, sweaty horses, and homemade scones.

We'd set our ropes doubled on the ground, carefully load them up, throw the ropes over the hay, poke the ends through the loops, and draw them tight. We'd heave the loads on to our backs; mine small, Dad's so big that from behind I'd only be able to see his boots going off in the same direction as the bundle of hay.

Watching him move across the paddock, his hat pulled down, his pipe turned over, the wind and the rain belting into him so he must lean forward into the force of it, I was struck by his resolve, or his stubbornness, which I realized he had, no matter what the job or the situation; and I tried to think of a quotation he had written in Aunt Margaret's autograph book, something about doing things easily, like a tree blossoms after years of gathering strength.

Whenever I saw him carrying hay, I had the feeling he was testing himself to carry a little more, or to go a little longer, even though the rope would be cutting into his shoulder. And when he put his load down his fingers would be white where the rope had dug in. I have seen him manually straightening each finger and rubbing them to bring back the circulation.

Wood! I had almost forgotten it. I sorted out a bundle of small dry wood and took it up to the wood-box. I gave Hong a couple of bits to give to Mum and went out to the wood-heap to re-cover the stove wood and to take a barrow load, wet as it was, back to the house.

I looked down to the flat to see Dad throw out the last bit of hay, and, despite the rain, stand there to watch the cows

eat. Then he started off back to the house with the wind
behind him. He was swinging the end of the rope backwards
and forwards and I thought: he doesn't even care about it
raining.

I went inside and washed ready for breakfast. Mum's mood
still hadn't returned to normal, but at least the fire seemed to
be going all right when we heard Dad on the back verandah.

He came in at last, shutting out the weather, his face
shining from the cold rain, or a recent wash and rub. He was
smiling broadly and keeping one hand behind his back. As
he walked over to the stove, I could see he was holding a
bunch of flowers, a mixture of fuchsias and daisies, that I
recognized had come from the bushes growing by the path to
the workshop. Their petals were drooping and clinging from
the battering of the weather.

'Good morning, Ame,' he said. Mum held out a cheek
and, concentrating on the potatoes in the pan, mumbled a
'good morning'.

'Happy anniversary!' Dad said, and with a flourish pro-
duced the flowers dancing in a hand which was shaking off
the drips, a hand which was thick and brown and knuckled,
and more used to holding lumps of rock, or logs of wood.

Mum was obviously bewildered. The fire was burning
now. The porridge on the side was cooked and plopping
occasionally with little subterranean eruptions. The bacon
was cooked and keeping hot in the oven. The potatoes were
beginning to brown in the pan. Now, only the eggs to cook,
and the toast to make. But the anger over the wet wood
remained simmering. Somehow that must be accounted for.
The utter waste of time.

The anniversary!

As if someone had fired a gun at the doorway. It was true
of course. It was 13 May. It was their anniversary. And she
had not remembered. And the flowers. Perhaps when they
dried out a bit she could make something of them in a vase.

12

But it was the thought. The surprise.

'Oh, Kay,' was all she could say for the moment. Was all she dared to say. Looking at the polished face grinning at her. 'I'll get you some dry trousers,' she said then, hurrying from the room. 'You'll catch your death in those . . .'

DIDDIE LEE GOES FISHING

There were two things in the world Diddie Lee said he liked above all else: fishing and music. He was good at both; he was usually asked to accompany any visiting singer and once had accompanied Dame Nellie Melba. He liked golf too, I knew, because he often talked about his golf and I had seen him dressed up in his plus-fours and diamond-checked socks and tweed cap, his shanks looked too thin to take the weight of his round belly.

He hated the trading bank where he worked for a living but had long since learned to accept that work was a necessary and tiresome means of earning enough money to be able to do what you wanted to do in life. 'You would have to agree, Kay,' he said, 'that the percentage of people who find pleasure in their work would be very, very small indeed, much like you must detest, Kay, going out to milk cows at some ungodly hour in the morning, wet or fine.'

I wondered why he always called my father by his first name and my mother, Mrs Roberts; especially as my mother was almost always the one to pay money into their account at the bottom bank where Diddie Lee was the teller. And she used to laugh, but I thought it was rude, the way he would ignore her, well not altogether ignore, he would stop and look at her when she disagreed with something he had said, which she did quite often, then turn and address Dad, as if, because she was a woman, Mum didn't quite understand what he was saying.

Dad rarely bothered to argue, which, I suppose, was taken as agreement. He would sit in his armchair with his feet on the hearth and stare into the fire. He always seemed to have his pipe in his mouth, either cold or with lazy wisps of smoke curling up from the bowl. There was something very friendly and permanent about Dad and his pipe. One of our birthday or Christmas presents for him was to gather dried, round rush stems, which we cut in lengths and tied in bundles. These were kept in a box and from time to time transferred into a tin, which hung on a nail on the side of the mantelpiece. Whenever he wanted time to think, if cornered into making a statement or answering a question, he would take a taper from the tin, lean forward to get a light from the fire, suck the huge flame into the bowl of his pipe and pinch the flame out with his fingers before speaking.

I knew Dad would have agreed with what Mum had said about finding pleasure in work, but I wasn't sure whether her objection to what Diddie Lee had said was genuine or simply to defend their situation, because their work, whether they liked it or not, was their life. The difference between my parents and others on a regular wage was that Mum and Dad might work for weeks sometimes and receive no payment whatever. In fact only a few days ago, I knew, my father had received a bill from his local merchant for the cost of freight and merchant's commission for loss on a consignment of ten tons of potatoes shipped to Sydney and sold by Doust and Rabbidge at a give-away price.

'Weeks of work had gone into earning a loss like that!' My mother was angry. 'It was wrong. Something had to be done. Why should the only one to lose be the farmer? What about the suppliers of seed potatoes, manures, bags, potato forks, needles and twine, the carriers, the railway, the merchants, the shipping companies, the retail shops in Sydney.

'Didn't the farmer pay for all? And if the price were down; if there were a glut and the merchants wouldn't accept the consignment; if the weather were such that it caused the whole shipment to be lost through blight, who then, might I ask, was the only one to suffer loss? Why, the farmer!'

And my father would sit and listen and say: Yes, and yes, and yes, and suck on a pipe which he kept lighting and stare into the fire; or in the daytime, take his billy of cold tea and a sandwich wrapped in newspaper and go off to the paddock where he could work and forget about all those others who didn't understand – who didn't care. And after a time he didn't care any more either – only lost himself in wondering the truth of what Ruskin said: The first of all English games is making money, an all-absorbing game, and we knock each other down oftener in playing at that, than at football – and he would purse his lips and make squeaky noises to bring a pair of cranky fantails to fly down to investigate him from the hedge, and even to settle for a moment on the end of his fork handle; or he would suddenly feel a zephyr touch his left ear and know there was a change in the weather, and look up to the sky to see the layers of cloud crossing each other. And work would become an ordering of body muscles – leaving the mind to wander, to flit like a moth, touching here, touching there, settling, taking off, tasting nectar, ignoring the bitter and the repulsive.

The man, arrogantly content, (now he has forgotten the loss on the potatoes) in knowing that when he returns home, there will be a wholesome meal of vegetables from the garden, and meat from a fowl, or an old ewe, or rabbits or fish the children have caught; and clean clothes, patched and mended and mended again perhaps, and a warm house, and a bed, and a woman who worried about all these things, and who loved him. And God, how he loved her! He couldn't imagine how he could live without her. And if a thought like that crept into his mind he would throw it out.

As for Diddie Lee. He would talk himself out in a while. Then someone would say: what about playing something for us. , We, the children, sat listening, turning our heads from one speaker to another, knowing that our evening routine had been disrupted. Tonight there would be no Bible reading, no reading from a novel. But it was a welcome change. We all were able to imagine in our minds the drama of Diddie Lee's adventure, which had started early in the afternoon when he had driven his shiny new A model Ford down the paddock and parked it by our garden fence.

Diddie Lee quite often came to fish in our river. Normally he would have spent the afternoon fishing, returned with several trout, one of which he would have insisted my mother should accept, stayed for a quick cup of tea and driven back to Wynyard. But not today!

He was late returning and Mum was even beginning to worry. 'He is never so late, Kay, do you think you should go searching for him?' But Dad wasn't concerned. 'The fish are biting. He would probably turn up with a bagful.'

The day's work was finished, we were all about to have our evening meal when there was a knock at the door. We heard Mum exclaim: 'Why, Mr Lee, whatever has happened? You have fallen in. Come into the bathroom. I shall get you a change of clothes.'

Fancy falling into the river! How could anyone fall into the river! 'He must have trodden on a rotten log,' Dad said, 'or been leaning over an undermined bank. It could happen to anybody.'

'We'll soon know,' Mum said, coming into the room with an armful of clothes. 'Kay, would you take him these. I'm afraid they won't be a very good fit – around the waist.' She was smiling. 'I'll serve up another dinner. It will take some time to dry out his clothes, enough for him to go home.' 'Isn't that my suit?' Dad said. 'Yes dear,' she was enjoying herself. 'Oh how I wish I had been there to see him go in.'

17

'Where were you exactly,' Dad asked, when we were well into the meal. 'Up past that row of pines.' He had lost his tweed cap in the fall, his rod had been broken and two of his fish had been spilled from his bag. 'And there I was,' he said, 'at the bottom of an eight foot bank in water up to my neck and that silly sheep standing there chewing and looking down at me.'

'You mean a sheep butted you into the river?' Mum was having difficulty keeping a straight face.

'I didn't see a thing – just felt this terrific thump on my bottom and the next I knew I was in the water.'

'That's Smyths' pet,' Dad said. We all knew about him. Diddie Lee wasn't the only one he had put in the river. And the previous week he had knocked poor old Mrs Windsor in the mud when she was collecting for the church. 'A pest of a thing –'

After dinner when we were clearing the table I heard Mr Lee say to Dad: 'Which is your chair, Kay?' When Dad told him he sat down in the only other armchair which was Mum's, and Mum shook her head at Dad, which meant: Don't worry, dear, let him have it.

He looked really comical when Mum suggested he might like to play the piano. He stood up, realizing how silly he must look with Dad's trousers not quite done up below his stomach which threatened to burst through the shirt, so crossed his hands over his paunch and waddled over to the piano stool.

'I must tell you about the fish,' he said, 'before I start playing.'

Mum had opened the bottle of wine which someone had given Dad last Christmas. Dad, who drank any alcoholic drink as if it were an unpalatable medicine, was able to see Mr Lee got most of the bottle, which left both men in good humour; Diddie Lee, even to the extent of being over-polite to Mum, and asking her to please choose what he should play, but first he would like to tell about the fish.

'A huge one, five or six pounds at least, facing upriver. I cast the fly beautifully so it settled just beyond the nose. It came slowly towards it ready to take –' His pantomimic representation of a fish with its mouth thrust forward and slightly open moving slowly up a full octave left Mum giggling, which seemed to please him immensely.

'Then at that moment the sheep butted me. I didn't know whether I had hooked that fish or not. I searched for the broken end of the rod, but it had been dragged down the river with the line and my good cap. I couldn't go back to the bank where I had been because that accursed sheep kept following me downstream. I was forced to take to the other bank, and about two hundred yards further on I noticed a part of my rod by a shallow beach on the other side of the river. And would you believe, there was the fish, at least six or seven pounds, hooked all right and snagged by a stick and lying quietly, except for an occasional flurry of movement. I thought, I'm soaked as it is, I shall wade across the river and hope I can at least save the fish. I got past the middle of the river with the current threatening to wash me off my feet when that beast appeared and walked slowly down to the beach with its eyes fixed on me. Not being sure whether the thing could swim, I stopped there watching it. It kept coming until it reached the water. The fish flashed from one side to another, the line snapped, and that beautiful monster was free. If I had had a gun I would have shot that sheep.'

Everyone now was laughing and Diddie Lee seemed as pleased as anyone that he had been the cause of such hilarity. 'Now, dear lady,' he said, 'your choice?'

Mum could hardly speak for laughing. 'Why, a little Schubert,' she said. 'How about *The Trout?*'

19

THE THRESHERS

For the children, the arrival of the drum was a highlight of the year; for the parents, a time of tensions.

The huge, steel-wheeled steam engine towed the threshing machine from property to property, from stack to stack; oats in sheaves roofed and architectural; peas, loose, in awkward mountains, part covered with a bag rug or tarpaulin weighted with stones or rails suspended on ropes.

Stacks waiting in corners of paddocks for the slow, relentless approach of the steel and steam monster, and for Ponto, the driver, arriving at last, jerking his signal (one long and two short) on the steam whistle, telling the district: the drum has arrived at Roberts's. As if they didn't already know, with the crunch of steel wheels on metal roads for miles back, and the rumble and rattle of wood, and metal screens, elevators, planks and chocks.

And Ponto, tall, big jawed and balding, with a hat, splotched with axle-grease and oil and charcoal sitting on the back of his head, acknowledging waves from farmers in paddocks, and kids rushing to the road (he liked kids, did Ponto) with a short, sharp toot.

Ponto liked being the driver of this power-horse, standing way up there behind the little steering wheel that seemed to turn revolution after revolution for almost nothing, and all those different levers: 'You've got to know what you're doin' – you've got to know – takes more'an a fool to drive one o'these, believe you me –'

Then the arrival of the motley – ('Tie yer dog up to the apple tree and lock up yer daughters, I say.' Old Clarrie said it every year) – but in dribs: on foot, bicycles, three on an old Indian and side-car, one on a pony, and finally Charlie Dunham in his T Ford to check over what the boys have done: digging in, chocks, levels; and nods at last, 'As long as the wind don't change!' 'Should we 'ave set 'er up on the other side in case it did, like?' That's Alf, who Charlie looks at and grins, because Alf (he might have a reputation for being a bit of a thief) is probably the best man he's got and so can do and say pretty much what he likes, the bloody fool.

Then Bern and Hong arrived with old Bonny, who knows all about traction engines and only pricks her tired ears when Ponto starts up; then the hum and whirr of wheels and pulleys and belts, and the shrill whistle all signal the start of threshing. Bonny stands on three and a bit legs with her head down, content to have stopped, until Ponto yells out: 'Over here boys, where I can reach her,' and directs the boys where to put the sledge with its load of water which they have poured with buckets from the creek into the iron water-butt which normally stood under the downpipe at the stable. They unhook her traces then and take her over to the log fence under the shade of the blackwood and ask one of the men on the stack to throw them down a sheaf as a treat for old Bonny. And they get two because the men don't care how many Bonny gets. And the boys say thanks and go off hugging a sheaf each and Bonny whinnies because she can smell them coming.

In no time it's morning teatime and here come the ladies: Bern's mother, his aunt from Melbourne, who comes over nearly every year, and Bern's sister Judy, who is still a girl, only a couple of years older than Bern and wears a big hat so she can hide her face from the rough young men on the stack, who made secret signs at each other. But it's what they are carrying which interests the men most: a bucket of hot tea and scones just out of the oven running with oodles of butter and homemade raspberry jam, and a tray covered with a teatowel, knotted at the top for a handle, which could be, would have to be, seeing where they are, those Anzacs made with wheat and rolled oats and coconut and golden syrup which Gilbert – Gusty Gilbert – swallows in two mouthfuls.

Then the machine is started again, the big crossed belts flapping until they settle in a low whine and the pitchers on the stack toss their sheaves over to the feeder who picks them up with his knife under the bands, carefully, and flip – the loose sheaf spews down the throat of the drum. And Charlie who is fiddling with the oil-can, or talking to Bern's father, or holding his horny palm under the stream of oats coming out of the chutes, to make sure there are no seconds coming out of the firsts and no firsts coming out of the seconds and none of either in the cavings, which the new kid, Billy, is dragging on the bag rug from under the drum over to the heap to be burnt later – 'All that bloody dust and rubbish – and get a move on, boy, for Christ sake' – and Charlie's ears are tuned to the groan of the drum, that it is not being overfed, and to the myriad of clips and claps and shuffles, even as he speaks with Bern's father he hears and registers where a noise is that shouldn't be.

And there's Paddy, two-handed Paddy, on the board feeding in as only an expert can. ('Leave him there for Christ sake, he's hopeless on the fork.' 'He's only hopeless on the fork, 'cause 'e don't want to lose 'is feedin' job.') And Jimmy and Trev and Pansy on the stack below the elevator where all the trash comes spewing out. Bern's father, who builds the best stacks in the district, watches out of the corner of his eye and shakes his head at their incompetence, but it's not his job, not this time, and anyway the stack only has to stand for a few weeks before Charlie is back with his press-gang to put the oat straw in bales.

And Alf and Snow and Nugget pitching. And Buck and big Andy on the bags, ramming the grain down into the corners with the long, round sticks, shiny as polished silver, and sewing, like they could with their eyes shut, and tossing the full bags, like they were filled with feathers, six high, and three high on the wagon when Bern's father was there with Bobbie to cart them down to the shed, because there might be a flood.

And all the time Billy the Kid kept going because he wanted the job, because, since his father had died and his mother with five kids, and Billy, the eldest at sixteen, he had to keep going to earn something for the family. Even though the wind was blowing the wrong way, the wrong way for Billy, that is, and his nose and eyes and ears and (yes, he could feel it) his arse were filled with spikey dust particles that itched; even though old Ponto gave him a hand occasionally, (good old Pont) Billy the Kid knew nothing would stop him holding on to his job until, maybe sooner or later, he would graduate to a job like the pitchers had up there out of the dust, flicking sheaves from one to the other, to the feeder, even feeding, maybe.

Then it's dinnertime, and eat, and drink gallons of tea, and (Bern's Mum's special) OT, a refreshing drink made with chillies and lemons, and, unless you're Alf or Jimmy, who never seem to have enough acting the tit, you lie on your back and wish you could stay there for a week. Then afternoon tea is come and gone and you're on the long shift before tea, which is when it's too bloody dark to see. And halfway through that shift, you were waiting for it, at least Alf was for sure, Nugget says he's got to go for a shit and jams his fork into the stack and slips over the side. As usual the others call him a bludger, but let him go, until Alf sees him cross over the log fence, and slips down after him, grabs Ponto's shovel, and, bent over, hurries after Nugget, but on this side, keeping an eye on the back of his head until he stops. Everyone sees then what Alf's up to and they watch him sneak his shovel over the fence and a minute or two later see it come back again with Nugget's curled up crap sitting plumb in the middle. Alf is back again before Nugget has got his trousers done up and everyone except the boss and Billy the Kid start cat-calling Nugget, who climbs back on the stack and gets in an argument. He was fair dinkum, 'He did have a shit, and if they didn't shut up he'd fuckin' prove it.' And they all stick their forks in the stack and follow Nugget down over the log fence, and stop to watch him look where he was sure it should be and wasn't. And they stand around listening to Nugget say he could of sworn he had a bloody shit and yet it wasn't there all right. And they watched him with his hands on his knees all bent over and shaking his head because it was unbelievable. And Alf slapped him on the shoulder, 'Don't you worry, mate, we all feel like you at times.' Then Charlie yells out, knowing they've had their fun, and in no time the old drum is humming as hard as ever. And Nugget, who still can't believe it, and keeps saying so under his breath, slugs away with his head down and knows there's something wrong somewhere, but he don't quite know where.

Back at the house, Lorna, she's about the best girl Bern's Mum ever had, comes bursting into the kitchen. She's been out at the woodheap. They heard the engine die a while ago and Lorna hears them coming before she can see them in the half light. Someone cusses because he has walked into something. And Lorna hears a whole string of oaths which send a shiver up her spine, and the others laugh. And Lorna, half excitement, half fear of being seen there on her own, grabs a piece of wood and bolts straight into the kitchen: 'They're nearly here,' she says. And Bern's Mum takes the wood out of Lorna's hand and jams it into the firebox and smiles at Lorna, one of those smiles that says: Look, I'm in a stew too. Calm yourself, girl, there's things to do. 'Are the basins on the back verandah? And the soap and towels?' And when Lorna nods: 'Then take this jug and get some cream. Loch should be separating by now; and full up, mind.'

Then they are washed and dried, and talking in low voices, and shy about coming in, until Ponto leads the way. (Charlie stops at the cowshed to talk while they finished off). Ponto is bright and cheery as he mostly is, and the others file in not looking except out of the side of their eyes; except at Lorna, who wonders which one it was who said all those awful words, and she won't look at them, and knows her neck and face are red. And as the first one slides along the stool by the wall a plate, piled so high you'd swear something would have to fall off, is dropped in front of him and Bern's Mum smiles and says, 'Hungry?' and Trev smiles back and says, 'Gee, thanks, looks good.' And Lorna is handing out plates too and the men are trying to catch her eye, and grinning, and making little cracks to each other, but Lorna won't look, just keeps handing out plates all piled up like the first one. And nobody says they don't eat this, or don't eat that, and after those first few mouthfuls they settle down to steady eating, holding their knives and forks, in tight clasped fists, between mouthfuls, with the butts on the table and the business ends in the air, as if they were members of some secret society. And when they had cleaned every speck of food off their plate they put their knife and fork crosswise with the heads together. And forever after when any of the children ate like that or did those things with their knife and fork Bern's Mum used to say: 'Come on now, eat nicely. You're eating like the threshers.'

Only Pansy, poor ol' Pansy, used to pick. He never ate the skin of the marrow, and the edge of his plate would be lined with little bits of potato peel, or a speck of black off a carrot or swede or a bit of cabbage leaf the wrong colour. And he looked like it too; so Bern's Dad said, poor old Pansy – wonder what his proper name is – as skinny as a rake, but a good steady worker for all that.

And one by one, the children, who had had their tea earlier and who had been inside by the fire with Auntie Vin, would find some excuse to go out to the kitchen and stand around taking everything in until Bern's Mum was able to shoo them back again in case they picked up a few more bad habits, or language – oh well, such is life.

After the pudding and the endless cups of tea and the warm-sitting-around-comfortable feeling, and Billy the Kid nearly falling asleep at the table, they all moved off to the stable, where Bern's Dad had set up a big heap of split bags and horse rugs and bits of tarpaulin and filled the stalls up with clean straw. All except Charlie who always went home and took Pansy; and Ponto who didn't live far away got a lift back with Charlie, who wanted to take Billy with him too, but Billy dug his heels in and stopped with the men because he wanted to be one of them.

And when Bern's Dad had taken them down to the stable and shown them where everything was, and the spade, in case they wanted to relieve themselves, and told them he didn't want them to smoke inside the stable because it could be dangerous, (which they didn't until he left), and had come back to the house, he found the whole pile of dirty dishes had been cleaned up and put away, and Lorna and Amy and Vin were sitting down at the table looking as if they had been washed up too, and sipping cups of tea. It was after their bedtime and Bern's Dad knew that he and Loch and Bob would have to be up at four o'clock in the morning to get the cows milked early; and Bern's Mum knew too that she had another big day coming and wouldn't sleep properly in the meantime and yet couldn't drag herself off to bed, and all the time, now that he had mentioned it, she would be wondering whether someone would fall asleep with a cigarette going and the stable and all the men and the chaffhouse full of chaff would all go up in smoke.

26

But it didn't.

The next day went like the first, except they finished up earlier than they had thought. And everybody was happy because they could go home for the night. And Bern's Dad was happy because it was a bumper crop, (ninety bushells to the acre, so he worked out, which Charlie said was the best he'd ever threshed). And there weren't any silly goings-on like there were at Medwin's, when, on the first night, Jimmy had woken to find the men had slipped some ropes over the rafters, tied the ends on to the corners of his horse trough, with him asleep in it, and hauled him and his bed to a couple of feet off the roof and about fifteen feet above the floor of the barn. So Jimmy had spent the second night out on the straw stack and Alf had let the bull out of its paddock, and it had spent the whole night, so it seemed, circumnavigating the stack and stopping every now and then to bore into it, so Jimmy got really mad, and got a little of his own back the following day by shoving a rat down the back of Alf's shirt which bit him a nasty bite on the bum.

Yes, everything went well, that second day. But Bern's Mum and Aunt Vin and Judy, and Lorna too, who carted the last afternoon tea up the paddock, arrived just when the men were about to take the last couple of layers off the stack and all the men had their trouser legs tied and the kids were there, including the neighbours', and all the dogs held back and ready to go, and Bern's Dad told the ladies to leave the things away from the stack as rats would be everywhere any minute now, so they missed the bashings with pitchforks and sticks and the grabbings of the dogs, but as they hurried back over the hill, they heard the whooping of the men.

And not long afterwards (an hour or two, time goes like that on a thresher gang), while the gang was lined up for its final meal down at the house, they all heard Ponto's whistle, which told the neighbours that Roberts's oats was finished.

A JAR OF RASPBERRY JAM

For the time of year it was warm. A dry spell, Bern's father had said, peering at a cloud, a big, shining, white one, which had slid quietly over Bassett's hill on its flat bottom, its top, dollops of mashed potato. Another fine day.

Bern wasn't interested in the weather, just then, although it was always easier in fine weather, you weren't stuck in the house or a shed.

He sneaked off without anyone seeing him except Vic who watched from under the quince tree to see if he was only going to the lavatory, saw he wasn't and followed him down past the calfshed, past the cowshed, along the hedge and over the railway to the bank, which looked north over the river to Ridge's and Edward's.

Bern sat on the grass amongst the ferns, which would make him hard to see by anyone over the river. The spaniel lay beside him, on his belly with his head resting on flat paws. His ears were touching the ground, his eyes were soft and dull, but followed the boy's slightest movement.

Bern reached a hand to lay it on the dog's shoulder. Only the eyes moved. If there was a problem, they would share it.

But there was no problem; not one you could write down or talk about. It wasn't as simple as that. An unease, an ache, that he couldn't describe; yet alleviated in a way just by sitting there, where he was, alone with the dog and everything familiar about him; like the relief of a poultice on a boil. But this was not something you could put your finger on, like you would touch a boil with the tips of your fingers and feel the core of hurt, an electric contact with the brain.

As he stared blankly across the river he began to focus on a vague something that caused his brows to lower and glower, and his mouth to pucker; an unattractive face, scowling and angry-looking. If you reminded him he could tell you how Mrs Webster had mistaken this look of deep concentration and stopped in mid-sentence to stare at him and say: Wipe that scowl off your face! And he had been amazed and said belligerently: I wasn't scowling. Don't dare answer me back, she had said. I wasn't scowling! (more belligerently) How dare you! Give me that cane! (pointing to the boy in the front desk). And Bern had jumped to his feet: I'll get it. And hurried down the aisle past the teacher, grabbed the cane from behind the piano and handed it to her, almost poked it at her, standing there angry and temporarily nonplussed. He could tell how she vented her anger by slashing at his hand and sending him out to the shelter-shed to wait until she told him to come back: how when school had finished and the others had gone home and she had imagined he had gone with them, he had stayed, still angry and pigheaded, in the sheltershed for an hour, until he had attracted her attention by dropping a board: how she had come out to the shed amazed and shocked to find him and ask him why he hadn't gone home when the others had left. And the culmination – his victory – You told me to stay until you called me.

If Mrs Webster had come across him sitting there on the bank with the dog she would have recognized that same ugly frown but it is possible that in his eyes she would have been just another nebulous object like the willows, the white gums and Ridge's barn on the hill (stuck there like an over-sized dunny).

29

It was to do with the Cullens. For all of Bern's twelve years the Cullens had been neighbours at the end of the road. And now the property had been purchased by the Shekletons.

Cullens! Mum, can we go up to Cullen's? Dad, do you want us to take that fork back to Cullen's? Or they had a fish to drop in. Or their mother, realizing the boys liked to see the Cullens, would ask them to take some little thing to them.

There was always a welcome there, perhaps because their only son, Frank, had been tragically drowned, and unmarried Stella was no longer living at home; perhaps, because the boys had no grandparents, they had adopted this old couple. Tom, who forever seemed to be singing tunelessly his deedle-um-de-de, and was apparently never busy, at least never too busy to stop and talk with the boys; and Clare, whose short, thick body was always clothed in a black and sombre dress, which contrasted markedly to the warm smile of welcome. 'Don't go far away, boys, and I'll have some scones out of the oven in two shakes,' or, 'Would you like to pick yourselves some mulberries? Or cherries? The starlings'll get them if you don't.'

There was the time when they were close to the house and the boys heard Mrs Cullen call: 'Tom! Tom! What do you think. The old goose has hatched out her goslings – nine of them.' 'Nine, did you say, Clare? Well, well, well, I'll go to beggery. I'll go to beggery.' It was another Cullen contribution to add to the boy's store of mimicry, as well as: 'Come and have a cuppa-tea, Tom.' 'O.K. Clare, deedle-um-de-de, deedle-um-de-de.'

The Cullens were poor, as every farmer in the district was poor, except for Mr Norton Smith, the manager of the Van Diemens Land Company, who owned 'Amberley', a beautiful and fertile property on Roberts's eastern boundary.

But Cullen's property was small and hilly and mostly covered with ferns and scrub. Mr Cullen grew a few potatoes, and oats for the horses, and turnips, and milked several cows, but since Frank's death he had little heart for the extra work required to halt the yearly advance of bracken, and rushes on the flats.

What little money they earned was barely enough to buy the few necessary items of food, and to allow the two old people to hold their heads erect on Sundays when the congregation's donations were read from the pulpit. Their Sunday clothes were used sparingly and with extreme care; they were the same they had been wearing for twenty years or more. Their clothes, like the house, the sheds, the horses' harness, and the water tank (which sprouted countless bits of rag and tarred wooden plugs) in spite of constant care and attention, were deteriorating to the point where they were becoming gradually unserviceable.

Notwithstanding all these problems, the Cullens were able to take pity on Old Jim, who they found destitute and sick, lying on the side of the road, to take him home with them, where he lived for years in Cullen's hut.

Yes, Bern knew, it was to do with the Cullens. There had been deaths in the district, plenty of them: old people, babies, a young man he hardly knew had pulled his gun through a fence and shot himself. None of these deaths had caused him pain. Old Jim had died. But then Mr Cullen. It was Bern's first real feeling of sadness, of loss – much more, (although he would never admit it) than the sadness he had felt when his aunt, his mother's sister, had died. The aunt who had painted the picture hanging in the hall, and who had carved the breadboard and the breadknife handle, but who he had barely known.

'Poor Mr Cullen has died,' his mother had told them one afternoon, when they came home from school. And he had gone down to the stable and climbed up to the loft. It was the first time he had cried over someone's death. He thought how Mr Cullen, a few weeks earlier, had taken him and

Harry into the house to show them something that someone (was it Stella?) had given them: an His Master's Voice gramophone, which he had wound up and played for them.

The record was an old one which scratched, and went from loud to soft, a man who talked and sang and finished a monologue with the line: Yours to the last drop, George. Several times it was played for them and each time the old people kept their eyes fixed upon those of the boys, revelling in their attention and their smiling appreciation. It was a gift, even bigger and better than the scones and mulberries. 'Come back and hear it, any time,' they had said as the boys ran off to tell their family.

Then Mr Cullen had died. Simply and suddenly. The farm was sold and Mrs Cullen had gone to Wynyard to live.

Now, she too was dead. His mother had told him, told them all. She had died four days ago. And his father didn't know and had missed the funeral.

Only a few days before she died, on the Saturday, Bern and his mother had driven, with Star in the jinker, in to Wynyard to see her and to take her some eggs and vegetables. She was living in a tiny two-roomed cottage near the brickworks by the racecourse. Mrs Cullen was upset because she only had an open fire and wasn't able to bake scones for them. 'A man is coming next week,' she said, 'to put a camp-oven in for me.' She played the gramophone for them but only one record: 'Take a pair of sparkling eyes'. The other one, which the boys liked, had been broken in the move.

When they were leaving Mrs Cullen asked them to wait. She hobbled back up the dirt track and into the house and came out with a jar of raspberry jam. Bern's mother had kissed her wrinkled old cheek and as they drove off Bern noticed his mother had tears on her cheek, which she didn't wipe off.

Now Mrs Cullen was dead. There was only Stella left. And she was ten years older than Bern. He hardly knew her, apart from seeing her often on the road with Florence Smyth, riding double-dinked and bare-back on the piebald pony or cantering down the road with sox on her hands, in the winter, for gloves.

Bern stood up. Immediately Vic stood too and looked up at the boy as if to say: what will we do now? Bern scratched behind the floppy ear, 'Do you remember when Rover died, Vic?' he said. 'Of course you don't, you weren't even alive then.'

THE BARGAIN

The first morning of the holidays at the end of each school term they were not expected to get up early. Bern mostly did. Unless he'd had a bad night with asthma.

This morning he was early.

He slid out of bed on to the mat, picked up the bundle of clothes his mother had put ready for him on the box and hurried out to the kitchen on his toes. The board floors were cold. The linoleum in the kitchen was colder.

He threw his clothes on the floor and stood on them. He opened the fire-box and stood, soaking in the flush of warmth on his back and belly. He dressed then, cut himself a slice of bread, toasted it and spread it with pork dripping.

He pulled on his boots, walked out onto the verandah and stood on the back step looking down over the garden to the river flats.

The sun had just poked over the dip of Medwin's Hill. A heavy frost covered everything except for the brown willows following the course of the river.

Frost sat on the garden fence, the roof of the cowshed, the branches of the walnut tree. Gravel on the path was pushed up on ice crystals. He could count the flattened footmarks made by his father earlier.

The landscape was white. Alight. Almost dazzling. Ruby reds, brilliants, droplets hanging on the wires or branches sparkling and disappearing as he leaned forward or back.

Loch's spaniel had sensed the boy was about and had left his bed of ferns in the woodshed to appear on the path below the steps. He looked up expectantly, waiting, wagging his short tail.

Bern laughed. The day, the dog, the hot toast and the pork dripping made him feel good. He broke off a corner of the toast and tossed it above the dog's head, and laughed again as the dog leapt and his jaws clamped on to the crust. 'All right, Vic,' Bern said. 'We'll go for a shot.' He went back into the kitchen and came out carrying the rifle and pocketing a few .22 bullets.

The boy and the dog walked down the path and out the back gate.

Bonny, standing by the ivy stump, whinnied softly. Bern detoured to the stable, leaned his rifle against the wall and went inside to get an armful of hay. Vic, sensing a rat hunt, immediately went snuffling and scratching at the chaff-house door. 'Rats!' Bern teased.

The dog growled and tore frantically and vainly at the base of the door, but followed the boy out with his armful of hay.

Bonny was waiting and tugged at the loose hay even before Bern could hand her any. He dropped the bundle on the ground and scratched the white star between her eyes. Before collecting his rifle Bern noticed the ice on the water-butt. He levered a stone out of the frozen earth and thumped the thick ice until it splintered. He picked out several spears of ice, leaving a jagged hole. 'There you are Bonny,' he said, 'you can have a drink now.' But Bonny wasn't interested. She didn't even look.

They went off then, the two of them, behind the cow-shed, in case Bern's father saw them and thought up something the boy could better be doing. They had stopped for a minute behind the elder tree when the back door of the shed opened and big Ginger walked out to join the cows which had already been milked.

He didn't move until his father had baled up another cow from the yard and until he heard the streams of milk hitting the bottom of an empty bucket, to be sure.

He could feel the cold seeping through into his toes and hands. He was pleased to move off and so too was the dog. They ran, leaving two sets of tracks on the white grass, cutting across those the cows had made. By the cypresses he came upon heaps of fresh dung near where the herd had been resting until driven back to the cowyard for milking.

Vic was nosing around, scenting at the ground probably where Lass had walked when she rounded up the cows. He stretched his hind legs back and piddled in short squirts. Bern laughed. 'You should cock-a-d-leg,' he said. 'You're not a bitch.'

They walked through the plantation of trees, a favourite resting place for stock in rough weather. And where Loch always came to get manure for his garden and for his marrows and pumpkins which usually won prizes at the Wynyard Show.

Bern's father was always harping about shelter for stock and how it would do a lot of farmers good to change places with their stock for a night. 'How'd you like to go home to a house with barbed-wire walls and the sky for a roof?' They had all laughed at that, it was so cranky to even think of it.

'You can laugh,' he said, when the rain was belting down on the iron roof so hard you had to speak loudly to be heard; and the wind was screaming through the trees outside, and the crack under the door, and their mother was saying nothing much but going in to get another saucepan to put under a new drip in the passage. 'You can laugh, but what would it be like to be a calf in a yard with no shed, and not even a couple of ferns against the fence?'

Of course they all had to agree with him and willingly

helped when he wanted to plant out another patch of shelter trees.

But there were problems. Unless the plants were soon protected the rabbits and hares would nip them off. As they couldn't afford to buy wire netting, or even old bags, there were only two things they could do: either cut about a dozen sticks for each tree, or have a campaign to get rid of the rabbits and hares.

Bern recalled how angry his father was, in fact how angry they all were when a few weeks previously they had spent ages cleaning out the rabbits with ferrets and traps and filling in the burrows near where they were going to plant a hedge, only to find they had suffered almost a total loss of trees.

The day had come when the guard fence had been erected and the trees planted and watered. They had all looked so tall and healthy standing there behind the new fence. 'All they've got to do now,' their father had said, admiring their handiwork, 'is grow.'

But the following morning Loch had brought the news. The trees had all been cut off a handspan above the ground, all but three. At first, nobody would believe him. 'How could they be gone? Hadn't they got rid of the nearby rabbits? They would have to cross several paddocks to get to them.'

'Yes, Dad,' Loch said. 'Cut off and lying on the ground beside the plant.'

'Hmmmm. I think I know –'

'Surely, Kay,' their mother said, 'you're not suggesting someone around here would do such a terrible thing?'

'Not someone, Ame, something. Hares! Blasted hares!'

He was angry. They all knew that, because he never swore: blast was the nearest he ever got. 'I've known it to happen before. They're obsessed with the preservation of their territory and regard young trees as a threat. Plant a young tree in the bush and they'll leave it alone, plant it on their feeding ground and they'll lop it off, clean as you would with a knife. Oh well, it's war on hares before we replant that lot.'

And war it was! The Watts and the Parkers came over the following Saturday with their beagles and greyhounds and their guns and bagged eleven hares in the afternoon.

Bern walked through the grove of cypresses. There was no sign of frost under the thick canopy of branches. The mulch of decayed cypress droppings and cowdung was soft and loose.

He stopped on the edge of the grove, Vic, as always, right on his heels. Two rabbits were sitting near the railway embankment, but too far away to shoot. 'We'll leave those until we come back,' he said to the spaniel. 'Let's have a look along the edge of the spuds on the other side of the line.'

He loaded the rifle, leaving it uncocked, and walked down towards the long bridge, which had been erected to allow floodwaters to pass beneath. He stopped under the end of the bridge and looked up at the massive, wooden girders which joined a pair of piles. He remembered how scared he had been that first time when Frank and Loch had kidded him into lying with them on the top of the girders while the train thundered overhead, the wheels no more than a yard above them, and bits of gravel shaking through the cracks in the decking on to the back of his neck. He could smile about it now, but it was still a bit scary.

He sneaked through the fence, careful not to make a sound. He cocked the rifle, held it ready to shoot and eased forward around the abutment. Several times he had shot a rabbit squatting on the edge of the potatoes.

They saw each other at the same moment. The boy was so surprised he remained stationary staring along the barrel at the man.

'Put that down!'

Bern lowered the rifle. He recognized Jim, the tramp, who

walked the line about three times a year and always stayed in King's hut up near the bush, sometimes for one, two, or three weeks, if there was enough food about, and, as Bern's father said, as long as no one offered him any work.

'Come here, boy,' he said.

Bern walked up to stand near the man who was still on his knees, a butt of potatoes beside him. Vic followed close behind the boy, growling, his neck hair bristling.

'Does your dad let you point that thing at people?'

'I was looking for rabbits.'

'You reckon I look like a rabbit?' The old man wasn't angry. He was smiling even, showing a mouth that was a mass of yellow and black teeth. 'You're a young Roberts, ain't you, boy?'

Bern nodded.

'Your dad wouldn't like to know you go pointin' rifles at people, would 'e?'

Bern shook his head.

'Then I'll tell you what. Let's have a secret, just you an' me,' and nodding at Vic, 'and your old dog. I'll say nothin' about you pointin' the rifle at me, and near stickin' a bullet through me fer Gawd's sake, an' you say nothin' about these few spuds 'ere, eh?'

'All right,' Bern said in a small voice.

'Good lad.' Jim picked up the butt of potatoes and held out his hand. 'Then shake on it. An' don't forget, now. It's a bargain. We don't tell nobody.'

Bern watched him limping along the edge of the paddock; going back to his hut probably. He turned then and walked over to the river, his mind on old Jim and how he could have accidentally shot him. He turned several times to watch the man getting further and further away until he had finally disappeared in the railway cutting.

Around the bend in the river, Bern found a rabbit squatting with its back to him and facing the sun. He fired. The rabbit flew in the air, then began struggling towards the blackberries. 'Go Vic!' The dog raced along the bank and followed into the blackberries. A moment later there was a scuffle and a squeal and Vic came struggling back through the vines which threatened to tear at his nose and eyes and the rabbit he held clamped in his mouth.

'Good dog!' He dropped the rabbit at the boy's feet, shook himself and sat looking pleased. 'Old Vic, doesn't need to talk. You know what he's saying without it,' Loch said once.

The excitement of getting a rabbit temporarily put the tramp out of the boy's mind, but now his wizened, brown face was back again, staring into the barrel of the rifle.

That's how they always hunted rabbits around corners, easing forwards with the rifle held ready to take a bead on a rabbit, that would run at the slightest movement.

Half an hour of walking and Bern saw only rabbits in the distance. They had been shot at regularly and were gun-shy. Sometimes as he passed cover he would hear the foot thumping signal for danger and the dog would look questioningly up at the boy: I know he's in the mouth of his burrow and if you like I'll go and dig him out. It would only take an hour or two. And so it would. Many the time, for something better to do, Scrub and Hong and Vic had spent ages gradually working their way down to the end of a burrow. And Vic, on his side, panting, growling biting at roots, flinging dirt far back behind with his great claws, or into your face if you happened to be there. But not today, Vic.

Bern cut up through Norton Smith's corner past Frank's garden but no more rabbits. He was feeling confused and depressed now.

His father had always been strict about rules: how to use a rifle. Never point a gun or a rifle at anyone. It's always the unloaded one that kills someone. Which was crazy, of course, but they all knew what he meant.

As for shooting a person! Bern knew he would never do

that. He couldn't. Well, he didn't, did he? But the thought of suddenly seeing a man in the sights, and he, with his finger curled around the trigger. It made him shudder.

He wandered up past the stable. Bonny was standing with her bottom backed into the ivy stump, enjoying the sun. He angled across to stop under her neck, with a rifle in one hand, a rabbit in the other. She rested her head on the boy's shoulder and blew nostrils of steam against his neck.

He laughed and rubbed his head against her nose. She didn't move when he walked away. She was too comfortable.

He opened the garden gate with his rabbit hand, let it slam behind him and ran up the path.

Drop the rabbit on the path beside the bottom step; check the .22 to make doubly sure there was no bullet in the breech; lean the rifle against the chimney corner; make sure Vic was lying there beside the rabbit so that neither the cat nor the cattle dog could touch it (both of them nosing around).

He was hanging his jacket up on a nail on the verandah when his mother came out with a dish of warm water and a smile. 'Here wash your hands in this. I see you got me a rabbit.'

It was good to be home. He could smell bacon cooking and he knew that there would still be enough porridge left steaming in the pot on the side of the stove.

He could hear the clatter of plates and bits of conversation come flying out the door, and as he entered, a chorus of questions and answers:

'How many did you get?'

'He only got one. I saw it.'

'How many shots did you have?'

'I bet he didn't shoot it. I bet Vic caught it.'

'Come on,' his mother said, 'a plate of porridge will warm the cockles.'

He stood there grinning, his damp hair on end where the

water had touched it. He took the bowl from his mother, holding his cupped hands down the sides and feeling the warmth soak in. He dribbled on a spoonful of golden syrup, making thin concentric circles and crossing them with a star pattern. Over the top he poured the cream-rich milk, milk which had spent the night in Dinah's udder, down under the cypresses – always Dinah's, because she was the only Jersey in the herd.

'I've got a job for you and Henry afterwards,' their father said. 'I saw some smoke coming out of the chimney of King's hut. That would mean old Jim is back. What about taking him a butt of potatoes and a few swedes. It might stop the old reprobate from sneaking down to bandicoot some of ours?'

'And if you skin and clean the rabbit, I'll wrap it up, you could take that too. We've still got one in the safe,' said their mother. 'The poor old man – this cold weather. Wouldn't it be terrible, living on the track like he does?'

'He probably prefers it that way,' their father said. 'Anyway, boys, will you do that for us?'

Bern was bent over his plate, concentrating on his porridge, shovelling it in as if he were starving. 'Yes, Dad,' he said. And 'Yes, Mum. We'll go, won't we, Hong?'

THE DAY BOB LOST HIS HAT

My father employed Bob Jackson because he had a reputation as a good and tireless worker. Bob also turned out to be equally capable as a story-teller, a recounter of yarns and experiences. I never tired of listening to him, and sometimes the word pictures he painted grew vividly in my mind, until I felt I had actually been with him at the time, or even that I had shared his thoughts and emotions. So it was with:

Bob took the lid off the copper. The rain pelted in onto the boiling water. He filled a four gallon kerosene tin, and then another, and hurried, as fast as the filled buckets would allow, over to the hut. He put one bucket on the step, opened the door and carried the two buckets inside.

He slammed the door. One after the other, he emptied the buckets into the tub. The steam rose in a cloud and flattened out on the low ceiling. 'I won't be a minute,' Bob said, and walked out again into the night.

He kept as close as he could to the fence to dodge the mud and dipped both buckets into the horse trough. Inside again she was waiting for him. He tipped a bucket of cold into the tub, put it empty against the wall and hung the chaff-bag, that had been covering his head and back, above it on a nail. 'Might catch a few drips,' he said.

'A bit more cold, Bob,' Barbara said. He poured it in slowly while she tested it with her toes. She was stripped

43

ready to get in.

'You're certainly big enough,' Bob said, eyeing off her belly. Grinning, she patted herself, 'It'll get a lot bigger yet. I've still got six weeks to go.'

'Do you feel all right?' He watched her standing in the tub, kneel down, and sit on her heels. He was thinking of old Ginger; they had to dry her off early, she got so she kept getting stuck in the bail. 'I'm all right,' Barbara said. 'It just slows you down a bit.'

The hut was a small room built on the back of the workshop at the bottom of the garden. There was room enough inside for a double bed, a cupboard, a chair, a shelf, and space, below a row of nails for hanging clothes, to put the tub for the weekly bath.

Bob sat on a chair rolling a cigarette and waiting his turn. In her squatting position Barbara almost filled the tub. Bob found it hard to take his eyes of this young woman, his wife. There was something cosy about their present situation: breakfast and midday dinner with the family, tea at night on their own in the warm kitchen, and the hut to sleep in. Work for either of them was no problem. As long as they could remember they had had to work, and here they were both being paid, and all meals found.

Through a haze of cigarette smoke he watched her, standing now, reaching for a towel. 'It's still raining,' she said. 'It might be too wet tomorrow.'

'Wet or not, I reckon I'll still go, although the boss reckons it'll be fine. You haven't changed your mind about going?'

'No, even if it was fine I wouldn't go, jammed up in a carriage, all that way, and sitting around on the sand. No thanks, I'd be a lot happier lazing about here. If it's fine I might walk down to see Iris.'

It was fine; one of those glorious summer mornings when all the world is washed clean and sparkling. An hour before the train was due to leave, Bob had set off for the railway station, like a schoolboy with his lunch bag packed with meat and jam sandwiches and a bottle of raspberry vinegar. He too was sparkling: the toes of his boots, his face, the seat of his pants, the shoulders of his navy blue suit, the ruby red stud at the neck of his collarless shirt.

His steps on the railway sleepers were short and mincing. He stopped once, ready to run. He was sure he had heard a train whistling in the distance, but relaxed again; it could have been shunting on another carriage in Wynyard, seven miles away. Sounds travel on a morning like this. He grinned when he thought of that fool, Barefoot Barton, always showing off; how he used to ride on the buffers when shunting, jumping off at the last minute; always looked like he'd be caught and flattened, like that poor bastard was in Burnie, but he never was. They made him wear boots though, on duty, or else they were going to sack him. You'd see him going to and from work after that with the laces tied and the boots swinging from his neck.

Bob took off his felt hat and held it in his hand. It was too tight. He didn't want to wear it, but Barbara reckoned he'd need it at the beach, what with the glare off the sand, and she wouldn't let him wear the old one. The last time he had worn this one, the only time – no, it wasn't, he had worn it to Pat and Marie's wedding first, then he had worn it to poor old Mullie Mulligan's funeral, but that wasn't so bad, you had an excuse there every now and again to take it off. Wonder what happened to Mrs Mulligan. They sold up her farm for next to nothing; and the girl, what's-her-name, she was up the duff to that no-good bastard, Larry, who cleared out to Queensland. Not a bad girl that, Madge, that was her name – could have done all right there – might have finished up with the farm – thank gawd he didn't, though – too hilly and rough – nobody's ever done any good on that place – apart from that, she wasn't a patch on Barbara – wonder how

Barb is really, what it feels like to carry that weight around with you all the time – never complains, but she's like that, puts up with whatever's going – o'course, it's the only way, moaning never got nobody nowhere – look what a nong Dick Spry is, everything rosy until you ask him how he's goin', then gawd! talk about moan, he's got this, and got that, pains here, pains there – real bloody joke –

Hullo, the Miss Nortons are up and the fire goin'; wet wood too, by the colour of the smoke – should go over sometime and cut a bit of dry stuff for them; there's plenty about, hundreds of those old stumps – can't get better than that – Paddy's too bloody lazy – think on the devil, there he is the lazy ol' bastard; fancy just gettin' the cows in at this hour – one thing about old Kay, he's always up at sparrow fart.

'Where d'yer think you're goin', all toffed up?' Paddy's got a voice like a bull, and according to reputation, he's just as randy.

'G'day, Paddy. You break a leg or somethin'. What's holdin' you up?'

'That's all right for the likes of yous, what don't ave ter milk on a Sundy.'

Not a bad ol' bloke, Paddy, Irish as they come, and real good-hearted like his missus – s'pose you can't blame 'im if he swings the lead a bit.

'Where did yer get that bloody 'at, Bob?' Paddy says, so Bob wished he could throw it into the cattle creep. 'She's a real Charlie Chaplin job.' Bob ignored him but pulled the hat down over his forehead, knowing it was going to leave a red mark and if he left it there long enough he'd get a bad headache. 'You want to let your missus do the milkin' on her own this morning, Paddy, and come on down to Stanley with us. The train won't be in for half an hour – give you time to get dolled up.'

But standing there on the track to the cowshed, with her

shiny bucket and bag apron on, Paddy's missus had been listening. 'Cut that out, Bob. Don't go puttin silly ideas into 'is 'ead. The ol' reprobate's lazy enough as it is; what 'e needs is a bit of a push along t'do 'is work.'

'I'll give yer push along,' Paddy says, very loud, so Bob looks back to see if any of the Miss Nortons are outside, listening.

'You got no push left in yer,' says Paddy's missus and laughs that loud musical laugh that everybody in the district within earshot knows. 'Have a good day, Bob,' she says, and waves. And Bob waves back and laughs, thinking how he'll tell Barbara all about it when they're sitting in front of the stove after tea, when he comes home tonight.

By the time the Sunday special comes whistling and chuffing over the crossing, there's as big a crowd on the Flowerdale platform as Bob has ever seen. And according to the heads that are poking out the windows of all the six long carriages, there's not a lot of room to fit in everybody waiting, let alone all those who'll be lined up at every tinpot station between here and Stanley.

The guard jumped from his van on to the platform as the buffers clanged, one after the other, bringing the train to a final stop. 'Back here,' he was shouting. 'There's room back here.' And surprisingly, there was enough and room to spare.

Bob put his lunch on the luggage rack with the motley collection of gear already there. A quick glance around told him that the only person he knew was Ape, with that new girlfriend of his.

There was a window seat and Bob took it just before a red-headed bloke, who had been bending over talking to a big girl with an udder like old Dinah, went to sit back in it. Bob looked up to see the red-head looking at him. 'You're in my seat,' it said. 'Serves you right fer gettin' out of it,' another bloke, with a big grin on his face, said. 'Don't worry, Mick,' the big girl said, patting the seat beside her, 'there's plenty of

47

room here.'

'You can have it if you want,' Bob said.

'Come on,' she said, patting her hip. 'Come on, Mick.'

Bob could see which of the two she wanted sitting next to her.

'Take yer bloody 'at off, mate,' a man said along the row, 'I can't see out the bloody windy.'

Bob had temporarily forgotten his silly hat and stood up to toss it in the rack, and wished he could throw it out the window. He couldn't work out why he had ever bought the thing in the first place. It either sat on the top of his head making him look a real gawk, or he pulled it down so tight it left a red wale that lasted for hours. Just right, the bloke in the shop had said, they always stretch a bit. Bob had tried it on his knee but it never had.

In that second while Bob stood up, the red-headed bloke called Mick, slipped into the seat, leaving Bob standing, half-looking at the space next to Mick's girl, which seemed to be disappearing as he watched. But everything was decided for him. There was a short blast on the whistle and next second, without any warning, there was a jolt of the carriage which sent Bob sprawling onto the lap of Mick's girl. His embarrassment was saved by the spontaneous laughter of everyone except himself, and (as he then found out) Maggie. 'Hey, Maggie,' Mick said, 'I know you wanted him to sit beside yer, but no need ter hug 'im.'

'I hope I didn't hurt you,' Bob said, struggling to get off. He slid onto the seat beside her, easing away from her as far as possible until he felt his hip pressing into the hip of the girl next along, and she was returning the press, like he and Barbara used to do on the train when they were courting. He moved back a bit towards Maggie and she didn't seem too pleased about that so he sat forwards and put his hands on his knees.

Bob noticed when he looked at anybody now they gave

him a friendly grin and one bloke winked, one of those big winks you could hear, with the eye shut tight and the corner of the mouth moving up level with the nose.

'Good on yer, Jack,' the man said.

'I'm Bob,' Bob said, and winked back.

'And I'm Bill.'

Ape and his girl were grinning like fools.

Bob realized that by sitting forwards like he was he could see pretty well both sides, which wasn't bad. He saw Paddy and his missus standing on the cowyard fence and waving; and then he saw one of the Miss Nortons on the verandah waving a hanky. And before long he was nearly up to his place. 'That's where I work,' Bob said to anybody, and although he was jammed in like he was he waved, because there was Barbara at the door of the hut, and there was young Loch on the fence by the copper, and gawd yes, there was the other kids, he just caught a glimpse of them on the back verandah. He wasn't all that worried about them not being able to see him wave, because he knew there would be dozens of people waving all along the train with anything they could lay their hands on.

Then the river and the big bridge and someone saying: 'A bit of good fishing there, I reckon, ain't there, Bob?' 'Too right,' he said, 'and see that big steep bank; I was fishing there one day. I'd hooked a couple of beauties, trout, about two pound, and who'd come out from under the bridge but bloody Bob Holmes, the bailiff, and he says: "What are you fishing for?" I was nearly goin' to say, "for fun", but I didn't. I told him, blackfish. He knew I didn't have a licence for trout and he says: "Let's have a look in your bag." "All right," I tells him, and took me bag off and put it right up against the edge of the bank and stood back so's he'd have to stand between me and the river, about ten foot down, to look. And he wouldn't look. He had the wind up I'd push 'im in. And him not being able to swim an' all.'

'Good on yer, Jack,' Bill said.

And almost as soon as Bob finished his story he saw where they were and started again. 'See down over that there bank,' he said. 'That's where the big derailment was last year. Nobody hurt. Just the cattle. Talk about a mess. Truck after truck went spearin' down the bank there – all tangled up – you'd never believe you could crush them cattle trucks like they was and cattle bellowin', with broken backs, and legs, and horns, and blood everywhere. The boss and me went up with crowbars and axes and he shot all the worst of them.'

'Just there, was it?' The girl next to Bob on the other side from Maggie was half standing up screwing her neck up and around like that cormorant, what roosted on the dead black-wood by the big bridge, used to do in case someone with a gun was about. It was as if she could actually see the mess of twisted trucks, and blood, and hear the bellowing. Then she was down again, jammed up that bit closer to Bob, and smiled at him. 'I hope we don't have a derailment,' she said. And a few of the others agreed.

But Bob was still in his territory. And Bob always liked an audience. 'This is the steep bit we are coming to. Once you get past King's here the wheels often start to slip, special when it's frosty. Sometimes they've got to put sand under the wheels to get her to grip. But she won't slip today, only go slow, like.' And go slow it did. And slip it did too, which made Bob into a liar, or so he said. 'But some of them don't know how to drive,' Bob said. 'This bloke don't. I knew when he jerked like he did at Flowerdale. You've got to know when she's going to skid, and cut the power.'

'Nearly jerked yer off, did he, Jack?' Bill couldn't resist that. (That's how he was, his mouth was mostly a yard in front of his mind.) Then he coloured a bit, (because of the girls – and Ape was wetting himself in the corner), unwound his long body and stepped over to the window. 'I could walk as fast as this,' he said, 'and by the look of things it won't get any better until we get up into the bush. Hey, Mick, let's go up and ask the driver if 'e wants a bloody push.'

'All right,' Mick says. And the two of them open the door and jump down onto the track and run up the side of the carriages, and everybody is cheering and laughing, and Bill yells out, 'We'll come an' meet yers when yer get to Stanley.'

And the guard is hanging out of the van and yelling at them to get back and waving his hands, but Bill and Mick don't see or hear him because they're going the other way and there's too much noice, what with everybody hooling them on and the sound of the engine skidding. Then they're up there talking to the fireman and waiting for the carriages to snail up towards them, and they're making slow motions like pistons with their arms, and pretending to kick the wheels, and putting their shoulders down to push. And then the guard, who wasn't getting anywhere by yelling, jumped down and started to run up the train, and every window was filled with heads and arms and people cheering and Ape, who had his head out the top of the door-window and was laughing like a jackass, said, 'Jeez, you'd swear they was pissed,' and didn't even look around to see if the girls had been listening.

Then the guard got up to them and tapped Bill on the shoulder and Bill said something to Mick and the two of them stood up straight, and skinny as crowbars, and saluted like they was in the army or the boy scouts and marched back down the line towards the last carriage. Then Mick, at the last moment, broke off and picked a couple of dolly bush flowers and handed them up to Maggie whose top half was hanging out one of the windows. And Bill said, 'Good on yer, Jack.'

When Bill and Mick were climbing back in, Bob, who had given up trying to get to a window was telling anybody who wanted to listen how a few times when the mushrooms were on the flats, the goods train had pulled up and the guard and the driver and the fireman went gathering mushrooms, and once they got a bundle each of daffodils down by the white gates; but most everyone was listening to what Bill and Mick had to say. Then they heard the engine slowly pick up and whistle and the bushes on the side started to go past faster; but only for a while because they had to stop at Allens Siding to pick up another lot who would probably have to stand wherever they got in.

Then Myalla, and through the Sisters Hills, (where Bob said the cutting was the deepest in the southern hemisphere), then Hellyer and on to Black River and Wiltshire Junction. And every time they stopped, more people were crowding into carriages where there was no room left. And at Wiltshire, which was the last stop, Bob (who by this time was nursing the girl he had been sitting next to, and whose name was Jessie) couldn't see any of the scenery because the passageway between the seats was full of people standing, and the whistle went and the train jerked again like at Flowerdale and all the hangers-on went swaying into the ones who were sitting on others' knees. And a new bloke who was tall and skinny went front first into Jessie onto Bob's knee, and Jessie felt her nose dig hard into the man's crotch, and the man said, 'Bloody hell!' and Jessie started to giggle and grabbed her nose and looked at Bob, and couldn't stop giggling.

Then Ape was yelling as if he was at a football match and laughing like he would bust, because he was beside the window and saw the bloke come tearing out of the lavatory, doing his trousers up, and screaming out, 'Hey, wait on, fer Christ sake!' as if the old train was going to take notice. And everyone saying, 'You can't get in here, mate!' Except Bill, who was barracking with Ape and saying, 'Good on yer, Jack!' until suddenly Jack was at his window and Bill changed his tune. 'There's no room in 'ere, Jack. We're packed in like sardines in a tin.' But probably because he knew it was his last chance, Jack took a dive and hung on to Bill's belt. 'Well I'll be the bloody oil.' The train was building up speed and Bill grabbed the bloke's coat, and somebody hauled on Bill and next thing they was all scrabbling on the floor like a tub of lobsters, all arms and legs. Laugh!

Bob tried to tell something to Jessie about how he remembered once there was so many people in a carriage – but she turned away because she was more interested in this new bloke, and there was so much noise and cussing, so Bob didn't bother then, he'd tell her later if he thought of it.

Then it seemed no time before they were pulling in to Stanley, and the cheering started again, and Bob caught a glimpse of the Nut, and wished they would hurry up and open the doors so they could all get out. Which happened. Even quicker than he had thought. Like everybody, he grabbed his lunch bag and started off with the crowd, in whatever direction they were going, because he didn't know, and he didn't know whether any one else did. And he thought of how once when the boss was loading sheep onto the *Defender* at Wynyard, and the hurdle of the pen broke and the whole mob went bolting down the wharf, and when they got to the end, one after the other, they took a jump in the air and landed about ten feet down in the water. But he didn't reckon people would be as silly as that. There was another story he must remember to tell the crowd on the way back.

But someone did know where they were going, for before long the stretch of sand, someone said was Godfrey's Beach, came in sight and lots of them started to run. But Bob didn't, he would get there soon enough. He saw Jessie not far in front of him with that new bloke, Jack, or whatever his name was, and she was hanging on to him like she had known him for years. Then suddenly this big hand fell on his shoulder and Bob took one look at the size of the hand and knew it would have to be the Ape's. And Ape said, 'Jeez, mate, I've been trying ter catch up with yer. Here's yer hat, you forgot it.' And Bob thanked him and cursed under his breath, because he had aimed to get a different carriage on the way back, and then tell Barbara someone must have pinched it.

'Jeez,' Ape said, 'wasn't it a bloody circus? I wouldn't 'a

missed it fer anything. An' that bloke at Wiltshire, reckonin' he was the bloody oil.' And Ape laughed so that everyone within two chains around looked to see what was so funny and could only see Ape nearly pissing himself.

Bob pulled the hat down on his head, because he didn't look so odd that way, and walked down with Ape and Ape's new girl, whose name turned out to be Bertha, but who said she usually got Bertie, which sounded like a boy's name, but wasn't, no more than Billie or Bobbie, which were girl's names too.

They sat on the edge of the sand dunes because, as Bob said, it's a good idea to see what's organized first, there's usually races and that at one end and swimmin' and that at the other. And that was how it was, just as Bob had said.

There was an ordinary hundred yards, and a three-legged race, and a piggy-back race, which Bill won with Jessie hanging on his back like a limpet, (which was a bit of a mystery to Bob, for where had that Jack bloke suddenly got to). And Mick and Maggie came in last, which was no surprise because Mick was handicapped, what with Maggie being so big and with her dugs, one each side of Mick's head, and resting on his shoulders. And someone made a crack that if that bloke runnin' last got a bit thirsty, he only had to swing his head to one side or the other to get a mouthful; but he didn't say it loud enough for him to hear, because Mick was a redhead, and redheads had a reputation for being obstropolous.

And Ape went off to have a go at throwing the cricket ball, and bowling at the wicket, and stepping the chain; he was pretty good at all those things, Ape reckoned. But Bob said he'd wait for the tug-of-war. He didn't mind being dragged along with his heels stuck in the sand. He remembered that time when they had a real tussle at the Waratah Carnival and they was pullin', first this way, then that, for over an hour before the other side packed it in.

He rolled his trousers up and went down to the edge of the

sea where the little waves were coming almost up to his knees, when they were coming in, and going right back so that he was walking on wet sand, when they were going out. The water felt good on his feet.

The day was hot enough, but there was a breeze springing up. Bob was getting a headache, so he walked along the beach a bit and lifted this black monstrosity on his head, and the wind, his new ally, swooped on it and sent it bowling along the beach on its rim.

His natural reaction was to run after it, and he did run, but a new gust sent it flying and he stopped. Smiling. Good riddance; as it went bobbing up and down on the water and moved further out from the beach.

He was standing there with the sea water swishing backwards and forwards on his legs and didn't see the young man until he touched Bob's arm. 'Would you like me to swim out and get it for you?' He was in swimming togs and deep brown to just above the elbows, and his face and neck and that V in front where he kept his shirt open was brown, and the rest of his body was as white as a Sunday shirt and Bob was thinking: damn him, I don't want my bloody hat back. But thinking quickly, like he mostly did, he said, 'Looks like there might be a bit of a undertow there. I know a bloke got washed out to sea in a undertow, at Doctor's Rocks that were, an' he was a good swimmer too. It was just lucky there was a boat out there at the time an' saved him. Anyways it's got a big gash on it an' it's not worth chasing.'

The young man said, 'You don't want me to try then?'

'No – wouldn't bother. Did you come down on the train?' A change of subject might help.

He said he didn't and that they were Baptists, (and he pointed to a group up the beach) and they had had a baptism a little while ago, and that he was baptized, and so were three others.

'Did you go in the water – right under, like? Do they

actually dip you?' (Thinking of the way they threw the Suffolks into the sheep dip and kept pushing them under with the pole every time they came up for a breath.) And the young man smiled and nodded. Then he asked, 'Are you a Christian?'

Bob didn't know what to say to that, sprung on him like it was out of the blue, so he nodded. And the young bloke said, 'God bless you,' and started to move off back to his people. And Bob felt a bit guilty and called out after him, 'Er, thanks for offering to get my hat, but it wasn't any good,' and under his breath, so he wouldn't be telling this young bloke a real fib, he said, well, not to me anyways.

For a while he stood on the beach feeling his feet getting sucked into the sand every time the wave went out, and the sand squeezing up between his toes, and he wondered how long you'd have to stay in one place before the sand buried you. He looked up the beach at the Baptist who was just about back with his mob and he felt sorry he hadn't stopped to talk a bit longer, he could have told him about the time Aunt Maisie's hat (a brand new straw) blew off of her head down at the Wynyard regatta, and how the wind took it like a kite and dropped it a hundred yards away on the deck of a fishing boat, and the bloke on the boat, who was watching a pillow fight on a greasy pole, grabbed the hat and brought it back to Aunt Maisie, who gave him sixpence for his trouble, and the hat as good as ever it was. But probably it was better he didn't as this young bloke might have wanted him to give him sixpence too for getting his hat, which he didn't want back anyway.

He wandered slowly back along the shallow water, his trousers, wet now, and rolled above his bony knees. He wished he could swim and could go out to where there were about twenty or thirty people fooling in water up to their necks, or better still to be able to enter in one of the swimming races around the yellow buoy, anchored, what seemed, a mile out to sea.

Someone was calling for those interested in a tug-of-war. Bob wasn't. Not now, with his head still banging away. He walked along the beach to where he could see Ape and Bertha beside a boobialla. He kicked his feet into the hot sand so that it squeaked like a kitten with each step.

'Where's yer hat, mate?' was the first thing Ape said, when Bob sat down beside them and pulled out his bottle and sandwiches.

'Gone,' Bob said, 'out to bloody sea.' As if it was the natural thing for hats to want to do. And to change the subject, 'How'd you go, Ape?'

'He won throwing the cricket ball,' Bertie said.

'I always do, don't I, Bob?' Ape said.

'I reckon. But ain't you going in the tug-of-war?'

'We thought we might see if we could find a quiet spot up past them bushes so's we can have a bit of a sleep, hey Bertie. This sea air knocks yer about a bit, an' throwin' that cricket ball –'

'Oh, Ape,' Bertie giggled. 'You are a one.'

'I might have a lie here out of the wind for a while,' Bob said. And did. Longer than he thought. The whistle woke him and for a minute he thought he might have missed the train. But it was only a warning whistle to get everyone starting back to the station.

It was near enough to dark when Bob walked into the kitchen.

'There you are,' Barbara said. 'Just right. I guessed you'd be back here half an hour after the train went down. Now get that into you and tell me all about it.'

There was so much to tell. 'Ape's got another girlfriend. And I'm not sure that he didn't miss the train, coming back. He wasn't in my carriage and he didn't get off at Flowerdale.'

'That Ape. I pity any girl who gets tied up with him.'

'Ape's all right. But you wouldn't believe, there was a kid

57

come back with us, young bloke, about twenty, from Parrawe. You know, he'd never been to the sea before and he kept looking at a bottle of something, which made Bill somebody-or-other, real funny bloke, ask what he had in it, and he told him — sea water. "I'm going to take it home t'show me brothers and tell 'em about how the tide comes in an' goes out an' that."

'"Good on yer, Jack," Bill says. He calls everybody, Jack, but it turns• out it was his real name anyway. If you call everybody by one name all the time, like Bill does, you got t' be right sometime. Anyway Bill asks him questions about where he comes from and that, like, then, sort of casual, he says, "How full 'ave you got it, Jack?" and Jack says, "Right up t'the cork." And Bill sits up real quick and says to anybody, "Hey, what's the time?" and someone tells him it's after six. And we're all wondering what he's on about wanting to know the time, when Bill slaps his cheek with his hand and says, "After bloody six. Jesus!" and his mouth opens, and we're all wondering, knowing there's something pretty wrong and someone says, "What's bloody up, Bill," and Bill says, "I'll tell you what's bloody up. The tide's due to start comin' in any minute now, and when it does, there's nothin' will stop it. There was a bloke, King Canute in England, once tried to, an' a lot o' good 'e did, I don't think. I tell yer it'll blow that bloody bottle ter smithereens an' us as well." And the young bloke panics and says, "If I tips half of it out, will it be orlright?" And Bill nods. And Jack does. And we couldn't believe it and tried to hide our gigglin' behind our hands, except Bill, who sits back sort of limp, and real serious like, wiping his forehead with his sleeve, and says, "Good on yer, Jack. You'll do me, Jack." Then someone cracked a joke that wasn't funny and we all busted ourselves. You know. You can't believe it. Only twenty miles or so from the sea an' never been there before —'

'I suppose it's funny,' Barbara says, 'but it's real cruel too, to treat the poor boy like that. Just because he's never had a chance. Anyway, come on, eat up, everything will be cold. And where's your good hat? I didn't see you with it.'

'Oh yes, my hat,' Bob said, taking a big mouthful, so he'd have time to think. 'My word, this is beautiful. I didn't realize how hungry I was.' And another mouthful. While Barbara waited. Knowing she would never see that hat again and trying to remember just how much it cost at the Don Store.

'You just wouldn't believe –' Bob began.

But Barbara knew she would. There'd be no reason not to. It meant another hat, that was all. And just at the time she was going to suggest they used that bit of money they had saved up to buy those baby clothes she was looking at last week at Miss Wright's.

Buying a Car

She stood in the garden. Smiling. Watching him walk up the track to the red gate. He turned there. Saw her. And waved.

She watched him disappear over the hill.

She continued to stand in the garden. The sun was warm. She was no longer smiling. She reached down to pinch off several dead flowers from a nasturtium which had climbed up the stone wall onto the pickets.

Still she stood.

But frowning into the nowhere.

> Something there comes and touches me
> When gay my draught is lifted up;
> That eerie hand upon my arm
> The wine spills from my happy cup.

'Is that someone's poetry?'

'Bern! I didn't hear you —'

'I saw you standing there. I came across the lawn. Did you make that up?'

'I didn't realize I was speaking aloud.'

'Did you make it up?'

'No. Mary Fullerton wrote it.'

'Who is Mary Fullerton?'

'Your cousin. Mine really. What are you going to do?'

'Did she write much?'

'Poems. Essays. A couple of books. What are you going to do?'

'Nothing. I don't know. The others have gone down to get pinecones with Bonny and the sledge.'

'And you didn't want to go?'

'What does it mean: wine spills from my happy cup?'

She smiled and ruffled his hair – hair that stuck out naturally like bristles. Probably why he was called Scrub. You're not the only one can play that game, my boy, changing subjects. 'Would you like to come with me to Marshall's Lane to get some red ochre?' Funny how thoughts popped into her head. But she did need red ochre.

'I suppose.'

'You don't sound enthusiastic.'

'I'll come. I'll go and catch Star.'

'Good. You've made up my mind for me. I'll just finish washing the dishes.'

Her depression lifted. O sweetest melancholy. It seemed she couldn't even govern her moods; they must be subservient to the whims of her family. She sighed. Was it possible Kay would come back with a car?

Her initial excitement oscillated with a fear it was all a silly extravagance.

When Amy Hagan was a little girl she would temporarily solve her problems by plucking petals from a daisy flower: I will – I won't. I will – I won't. This year – next year – sometimes – never. Goodness, that was lives away! But it did work. Once. Who are you going to marry? Tinker – tailor – soldier – sailor – richman – poorman – beggarman – thief. Not those last two. Gentleman – farmer. Better still hyphenate them. Then she had won. Or had she? Of course. A family of five beautiful children. A loving husband who might be going to buy a car. Or mightn't. Was that the problem? There was no certainty. God? About anything. A beautiful crop of potatoes, perhaps worthless except for stock food and for them, of course. Butter prices worse than last year, or better? Telephone? Electric light? Car car car car or no car? At least when she was teaching she knew what she had. What she could buy. Before that? At home? Prizes all the way at school, and finally, *The Magazine of Art*, not so much the book, (yet that was still a treasured possession) the excitement, the family watching, her new dress, her short hair, her walk up the steps to the stage. Miss Amelia S. Hagan. Dux of the Ladies High School, Sale, 1893. She was a young lady with the world at her feet. People told her so.

The hopes. Desires. Disappointments. The almost fearful uncertainty, after twenty years, of her move into matrimony. The adoption of a life not her own. A small farmer's wife. Her will, ideas, ambitions, bent to conform to accepted standards. Bent, but not broken. She had not wholly accepted. She had refused to learn to milk cows. To work on the farm as most farmer's wives did. She chose her jobs. She too had wanted to write like her friends, Minnie Grant Bruce and Mary Fullerton. But there was no time. Not yet. With five children. At least she had kept up her annual visits to the mainland. Family. Friends. Relations. To bring back books and hand-on magazines, piles of them: *Illustrated London News*, *Punch*, *John o' London*, *The Bulletin*.

'Mum, I've got Star harnessed, would you help –'

'Right. I've finished here. I'll put some other shoes on and leave a note to say where we are.' The snails on the thorn – O joy, who cares about a car? Really. I do – I don't. I do – I don't. I do –

In no particular hurry, the three of them, Mother, Son, and Hop-along (the trinity), were able to idle up the three paddocks to the road, the mother chattering, wondering whether the boy's silence was because he was worn out after last night's asthma, or was it that inner contentment that his father had? She thought not. Not this time. He was more like her and had probably built up a castle of gloom in his mind which would dissipate as quickly and completely as the morning mist when the valley warmed. Steam on the bathroom mirror. Wait. Patience, my dear Amy!

Perhaps a little silence. The pair of them. Silence breeds contentment, her father used to say. Did he invent that or was he quoting someone? No matter. No talk gives time to think. And time to think gives worthful talk. Put that in your book of quotations, Mr Stevenson!

At least the boy appears to be content. Watching his fingers beat time on his knee to the clop of the horse's feet. The sound of the iron wheel rims on metal, the smell of horse. And harness. The glorious luxury of sitting. Of being in no hurry. Of being. All on a spur-of-the-moment decision. She would sing. A passing thought, with this silent boy beside her.

Unconsciously, she flipped the reins. And was immediately sorry, for the horse which had been expecting that, or a touch of the whip, from the moment they reached the road, began to trot. But she knew he would slow to a walk at the first hill.

The number of times she had been down this road. Down and back. Many more times than Kay. He always seemed to be able to find a reason why he couldn't go to Wynyard, or to wherever. She had accepted that. Much as she had accepted doing the accounts, that is, writing up the ledger, writing out cheques, but never signing anything. Dear me, no! That was man's work. It had nearly driven her to despair at first, not having the slightest idea what was essential equipment, what must be bought, while what she had considered to be essential for the running of the house had to wait. Always the farm took precedence.

In those early years a chunk of her savings had gone on things for the house, things that would otherwise not have been purchased. She found that Kay would happily accept a Spartan existence, and that would also be her lot. If she allowed it to happen.

But they had come to an early understanding. Dear Kay. Dear generous Kay. Once a year travel to Melbourne. On the *Oonah* no less. What a tub! (But she had been gallant in that dreadful mine distaster.) But roll! A sick mother wanting nothing but to die, having to nurse a sick child. Last year, no, the year before, you, my poor boy, sick, while tied to the wharf. A wonderful beginning! Dear Kay. Have I been a demanding wife? Is it just for me you are today looking at a car? You rarely care to go anywhere; but you must admit it is always you who must be reminded it is time we left for home. You enjoy being. But never going to be. Always enjoyed the evenings. The clean-up-and-dress evenings, the readings by the fire. In so many ways the perfect husband. That early morning cup with a finger of toast, before that last sweet sleep. Thoughtful. And gentle. That's it. Gentle. And understanding. Not like those great oafs she saw. Husband and son, with their legs spread-eagled in front of the stove, mid-morning, just because it was raining. And she, wife and mother, walking over them to stoke, to prepare their dinner. Logs! But not for the Roberts! Oh dear no, she and Kay read and discussed. Admittedly he was rutted to Ruskin, Thoreau, Emerson, Wells, but the lighter reading – for the children – he enjoyed that too.

Come on you cunning beast. And flipped the reins. Silence is golden. Don't speak yet, Bern. The river water making such perfect noises. Those tiny birds Kay called tits and silver eyes. The warm sun. The two of them, she and Kay alone, and something about to happen. She knew it. Will you marry me, Amy? There. He had said it. Such a simple question. But the effect an explosion. Explosion? That's too harsh. The bursting of a flower bud. She could hardly wait to tell Eva, who said she knew it would happen. Amy and Eva had held each other. And cried a little. Am I too old to have children?

'You know Bern, we are very lucky people, aren't we?' There was no need to answer, looking at her face so full of love and happiness. He did smile though. 'Come on, Star, just a little further.' Perhaps if your father does get the car – perhaps.

There was no difference as far as he could see but there must be, his mother had said so and she was usually right. 'Not there, Bern,' she said. 'Tip that out and come over here.'

He dragged his empty bag along the bank. 'Look it's a different colour and it feels different in your fingers. I'll show you. See. There's a strip, a seam I think they call it, running across here. It's some sort of oxide of iron mixed with earthy material, I think. Must ask your father. The Aborigines used it to paint their bodies. They didn't have fireplaces; not brick ones anyway. Sometimes I think it would be much simpler for us, but colder of course. And the mosquitoes. I don't think my skin is tough enough; in fact I know it's not. I'm such a softie. Just scrape it down here very carefully. We don't want any rubbish mixed with it. Get the idea?' She knew she was prattling again.

And for why? why? why? The boy is dreaming. Look at him. He's not seeing what he's doing. But thank God science has not discovered a probe to plumb the depths of our minds. What goes on inside that prickly head?

'That house, there, that's called Chambers.'

'What! What house? Oh, you mean Alexander's?'

'Chambers. That's what it's called.'

She looked at him standing there, holding the bag by one corner, staring at the house – large, old, unpainted, weatherboard, shingle roof. 'Who said so? I think Mrs Alexander lives there.'

'Dick Johnson. She does.'

'Well, he should know; at least his father would. He has lived around here all his life. But wait a moment, I believe I have heard Mrs Alexander was previously a Mrs Chambers.'

'She was.'

'You seem to know more than I do. Why the interest?'

'How old is she?'

'About ninety, I think.'

'That's what Dick said. Gee, that's old. It *is* right, what Judy said, that she has hens inside, and the floor is just dirt?'

'It's what Judith said. I imagine the only time she has been inside was when she called there because she had broken her bike chain. Anyway, we must get on with our work.'

'Could we make some excuse and go and have a look?'

'No, we certainly could not. And what if it is a dirt floor, and what if there are chickens inside. There must be thousands of places in the world like that – oh, Bern dear, look what you are doing! That's not ochre. That's dirt. Help me put my bag in the cart, will you? We'll tip yours out and start again. You're not thinking, are you – about what you're doing that is? Perhaps next time we want ochre we may ask your father to drive us here in the car.' (Let's try a little shock treatment.)

'Car! Did you say car?'

It works. 'I though that might spark you up a bit.'

'Is Dad going to buy a car?'

'He's gone to look at one, a second-hand one, but there's no guarantee he'll get it. Mr Lee was taking him to see it and to advise him. We won't know anything until tonight. But don't be disappointed if he doesn't get it. We weren't saying anything. It was going to be a surprise if he got it. But there I've let the chicken out of the coop. Now come on, help me with this lot.'

It worked. The boy's mind was captured by the idea. 'A car! Would it be like Mrs Webster's Buick? Or Glover's Chev? Or Honeyball's?'

'Who is Mr Honeyball, for goodness sake?'

'Honeyball. He is the man living at the beach. We could

hear him coming for miles.'

'Oh, when you were at Boat Harbour School. I know. He frightened poor old Star once on the road with his red bullet roaring, and his girl friend. Hair and scarves flying. Our's certainly wouldn't be like that, I hope. I know your father wouldn't be interested in that.'

What was she doing? Building up both their hopes! 'He probably won't be able to get what he wants. It would have to be a second-hand one, and cheap enough for us to afford. Don't be disappointed if we don't get one.'

'I reckon Dad will,' Bern said. 'When he wants something, he usually gets it.'

The milking was done. Everybody was cleaned up, ready and waiting for their meal and for news of the car. No longer was it a secret.

'Here comes Dad.' Loch had seen him come through the red gate at the top of the paddock. They all rushed to the window. He was carrying a bag of oranges and was holding one in his right hand and tossing it in the air and catching it, again and again.

'He didn't get it,' she said. 'He's got oranges instead.' Her voice was flat and lifeless, killing off their excitement. Why had she ever opened her big mouth? Why? 'Come on,' she said, 'let's sit down and be ready to eat the moment your father arrives. He will be exhausted. Judith, give me a hand to carry the dishes in.'

'I'll help,' Hong said. She turned on him almost angrily. 'Sit down when I tell you. We can manage.' But softened. 'Thankyou all the same. I want us all to be seated when your father comes in.'

They heard him go to the kitchen, then the bathroom. They were seated at the table when he walked in. He looked at the faces staring at him, silently, hopefully, waiting for whatever news he had to bring them. They know, he thought. Amy has told them why I went.

'You decided not to get it, Kay,' she said. Her voice lacked interest. She knew he didn't get it. She should have known he wouldn't. She should never have told the children. A stupid, unnecessary thing to do. The hopes. The disappointments.

'You know I went to look at a car?' He addressed the children.

Heads nodded.

'I bought a dozen oranges,' he said. 'What's more, I bought a second-hand 1930 model Rugby six-cylinder tourer.'

Standing there proud as a schoolboy who had just won a race. His family eager to hear more. And clamouring for it. His wife, loving him. Not because of the car. For the joy he always received in being the courier of welcome news – the birth of a new calf, the first daffodil, the finding of something lost, something treasured, the purchase of a car.

A PARCEL TO COLLECT

His initials were G G.

Talking to him or about him to grownups, we always said Mr G, but to us he was always Old Horse; yet he was probably no more than forty. He was what we called wiry; small and tough. His face was a deep brown and crinkled. I used to think it was dirt until I saw him on his back verandah one day, his face hidden in a lather of soap. I had called at the stationhouse for a parcel that Mum was expecting and there he was, with his cupped hands ready to dip into the tin dish.

He rinsed the soap off his face, tossed the water on the garden and grabbed the towel from the nail on the wall. He dried his face and hands before paying me any attention other than an initial squint of recognition through the lather of soap. His skin, I noticed, was the same deep leathery brown except that now it shone as if it has been polished.

'So young feller-me-lad an' what can I do fer you?'

He was always friendly, ready to tousle my hair if I was near enough, or to grin, not so much with his mouth but with his eyes, which actually sparkled. 'I like him,' I said at the table one day, when Bob said Horse was a lazy devil. 'George is all right,' my father said, lumping him into that middle category between he's a very fine person and a bit of a waster. 'Them fettlers are all a lazy bunch!' Bob always liked to have the last word.

'I've come to see if there's a parcel for Mum,' I said.

'Then we'll go and look.' He reached inside the back door and took a bundle of keys on a ring from a nail in the passage.

We walked over to the station together, Old Horse keeping up a constant stream of questions, or statements, 'I see your dad is puttin' a bridge over the creek.' 'They tell me your old cow lost her calf in the river yesterday.' 'See your mum had someone stayin' with her last week. Would that be her sister from Melbourne? I met her once last year when she was over. Nice woman.'

Everybody in the district seemed interested in what everybody else was doing. Some more than others. Mum said it was because few people read books and that it was necessary for everyone to be interested in something outside themselves. I know I spent a lot more time thinking about whatever book Mum was reading out loud to us at nights, like the next chapter of *Westward Ho* and what Amyas Leigh would do next, than about the doings of the neighbours.

After I had laboriously signed the consignment sheet and collected the parcel, and while we were walking back together towards the house, he stopped and, looking down at me, said, 'I know you wouldn't know anything about it, but someone has been busting the telephone cups up the line, and the powers that be are asking who done it. If you 'appen to 'ear of anyone like –'

I felt his dark eyes searching for mine, but perhaps that was my imagination. I knew my normally pale skin would be turning from pink to red. I dropped my head and heard his voice drawling on, '. . . that pole there is about the only pole on the line from 'ere to the river bridge which ain't got a chipped cup.'

I sneaked a look at him. He was looking up at the pole.

'Y' know when I was a kid, I reckon I would'a' been real good at bustin' them cups, not that I would'a' did it like.' He looked down at me, his eyes a-twinkle. 'Anyways, young feller-me-lad, I'd better go an' get me dinner, else she'll come screamin' after me with a big stick.'

By she I knew he meant Mrs G, a massive woman, twice the size of Old Horse, and kind. I couldn't imagine her ever screaming; or shouting even. She had a pleasant, soft voice, and, I was told, although I had never heard her, she had a lovely, deep singing voice and sang every Sunday in the Methodist church, which we didn't go to.

She appeared at that moment at their front door. We both turned when we heard her opening the door to see her almost filling the doorway. 'Hullo, Bern,' she said. 'I see you got your parcel.'

'Yes, Mrs G, thankyou.' And remembering what Mum had said about Mrs G always liking to know what's in a parcel, and how telling her, Mum said, was better than having her poke into the wrapping like Mrs B used to do before her, I said, 'Mum is expecting a parcel of hand-me-downs from my auntie in Hobart.'

She nodded and smiled.

'I was just telling 'im if I didn't get a 'urry on, you'd be out after me with a big stick,' Old Horse said, 'an' sure enough there y'are.'

'There's only one thing that'll bring him in in a hurry, Bern,' she said, laughing, 'and it's not a big stick.'

'Well, go on, tell the boy what it is.'

She was standing there with her legs apart and her huge, bare arms crossed over her chest. I was always fascinated by the size of those arms; her wrists were bigger than my legs above the knee, and where they met her hands, it was as if there were bands tied tight around her arms to stop the flesh or fat or whatever it was from running down into her hands and fingers, which were quite ordinary, well almost.

Before Mrs G could answer I made some excuse about having to get back to help Dad. Old Horse ruffled my hair.

'Go on,' he said, 'off you go. An' don't forget, if you see anyone bustin' telephone cups, you tell 'em, like I said, eh!'

I hurried up the line, not stopping until I knew I was out of sight. My mind kept jumping from the broken cups to Mrs G and back to the cups again. As far as those broken cups was concerned, it wasn't all my fault. Hong had smashed his share. As for Mrs G, the thought which kept creeping back into my mind was what she had meant when she said there was only one thing which would take Old Horse back inside in a hurry. It's funny, I thought, but all grownups seem to think kids were dumb. Just going on what I had picked up at school, I knew they must have been talking about sex. Then the problem I faced and couldn't easily get rid of was how it would be possible for Old Horse to have sex with Mrs G. As Clarrie Harris had once said, 'Old Horse on top of Mrs G would look like a pimple on a pumpkin.'

Just the thought of that then made me laugh. I picked up a stone, had a shy at a cup and missed, and then holding the parcel by the string I started to run: run one pole, walk one; and all the time as much as possible, without my feet touching anything but the steel rails.

I wondered whether there would be anything in the parcel for me. I bet there wouldn't be. It would be something for Judy. It usually was. I supposed, because she was the only girl in the family.

After a while I lost my balance and stopped. From where I was standing Norton's sheep dip was a narrow strip of water under the roof about thirty yards from me. I chose two good round stones. If I could land the first stone in the water there'd be something in the parcel for me; land the second one and neither Dad nor the powers that be would ever find out it was Hong and me who had busted the telephone cups.

The first stone hit the upright and bounced onto the long grass. The second one hit square in the middle of the strip of water.

What did I care about not getting anything in the parcel. It probably would have been some sissy thing like those Tussore silk shirts we got once before and all the kids had laughed at us. I took one more shot at a cup then ran as fast as I could, this time, without missing a single sleeper.

THE PEA GAME

'Watch this,' I said, 'a double barrel.' I had carefully loaded a pea into each nostril, and taking a deep breath, blew out through my nose. Hong said, 'Only one came out.'

It was the year of the big flood.

It had been raining intermittently for days, but on this day the river had risen enough to make the big flat into an island. It was what we had been waiting for. Frank and Loch had told us that they would take us rabbiting if the flood was big enough.

Rabbiting meant skins and skins meant money. It meant meat too, of course, meat for the table until we were thoroughly sick of it and carcases to be boiled up in the dairy copper for pigs and dogs. But it was skins we were paid for. The Chinaman was paying a shilling a dozen for good buck skins, incentive enough for us to risk a certain amount of danger and discomfort; particularly as almost our only other source of pocket money was from the sale of cocksfoot seed, the sheaves cut on roadsides or along fences or creek-beds on the farm and threshed with a flail.

Once I had unsuccessfully used my initiative to practise free enterprise and after packing two bags tight with dry ferns, which Mum found invaluable for starting fires, I had struggled home with them and offered them to her. She was really pleased until I had suggested she might like to pay me threepence a bag. She gave me a short lecture on being generous and working for each other and told me that if I didn't wish to give them to her (which of course would make her very happy) then I should take them back to the paddock where I had got them, which of course I didn't.

All morning we had watched with mounting excitement as the dirt-brown river swelled to overflow its banks, to fill the creeks and hollows, and at last to trickle over the tongue of land which, until then, had been a possible escape route for rabbits washed from their burrows along the river bank.

It was early afternoon when the five of us set off in the rain with a sugar bag and a stick each. We were soon soaked through, which, as always, was a relief, after the discomfort of water trickling down the spine.

We crossed a wide stretch of water about ankle depth and splashed each other with our sticks. Frank, who knew all there was to know about floods and chasing rabbits, cut a stick and hammered it into the ground so that it was a little above water level. 'When the water reaches the top of that stick,' he said, 'you three have gotta be off the island.' We nodded because we knew he knew, and if we didn't do as we were told he and Loch wouldn't let us come again.

Within minutes the chase was on. As the water rose rabbits were forced to leave the blackberry bushes lining the river bank. Not the usual fluffy, cocky, prick-eared rabbits we were used to seeing, but soaked and bedraggled, wild-eyed creatures, attempting to hide in a clump of grass, or under a fern even, bolting at the last moment if the savage, yelling, stick-wielding maniacs came too close.

For them there was no ultimate escape, except, in final panic, to fling themselves into the giddy current, to be carried off somewhere, anywhere – or to drown.

It was in an attempt to catch one that had taken to the water that Judy fell into a hole and was almost swept away after the rabbit. Fortunately, Loch was near enough to grab her, but it ended the chasing for the three of us.

We were sent off home and Judy, who was still feeling sorry for herself, was happy to do what Mum said: have a bath and go to bed.

Hong and I then had a bath, which lasted for an hour or so, then we were told to stay in the kitchen.

Mum had to walk a mile to the railway station to get a parcel. Dad had had his afternoon tea and had gone off to milk, leaving instructions, that as soon as Frank and Loch returned, they were to go and help him.

Neither Dad nor Mum had been in a very good mood. 'All the extra work,' Mum had complained when she picked up the three sets of dirty, wet clothes, 'and your two brothers and your father yet to come.'

I think she wanted an excuse to get out of the house, because when we suggested that we would go to the station for her, she said quite definitely that she would go, and suggested, unfairly, that we would probably go off chasing rabbits and forget about the station.

We always found it harder to amuse ourselves inside the house. Mum had told us to read, but we didn't feel like reading. We kept thinking of Frank and Loch still chasing rabbits, and how much money we could have made if only we could have been allowed to stay on.

Hong was poking about in the cupboard looking for a biscuit when he came across a jar of seed peas. 'I know,' he said. He was always like that. Ideas would suddenly hit him. Nothing had been further from his mind at that moment than having a competition to see who could blow a pea furthest out of his nose. Yet within one second of picking up the jar he had it all worked out, rules and all.

Actually he had plenty of ideas after I got the pea stuck up my nostril, but none of them worked out. Some of them I didn't try because I thought they would hurt too much: like shutting my eyes while he punched my nose. He thought that the pea would be sure to come out with the blood. After the pepper didn't work and blowing my nose under water in the wash-up dish, we went to see if Judy had any ideas.

She was sitting up in bed like a duchess, with books spread all around her. She probably thought we had gone in to see how she was, for as soon as we walked into the room, she put on that I'm-not-very-well look and put her hand up to her forehead.

'I've got a pea up my snout,' I said.

'Oh, go away,' she said, 'I'm still feeling a bit shocked.'

Hong and I looked at each other and then at her. 'He has,' Hong said.

'I have,' I said.

'Have you?' she said. 'Mum will be home soon. She'll get it out.' And she went on reading.

'It hurts,' I said. And started to cry.

Hong looked at me. He never cried. Not really. Unless he was nearly killed. I didn't want to cry, but I wanted to make my sister take notice.

She jumped out of bed and put an arm around my shoulder. 'Don't cry,' she said.

'It hurts,' I said.

'It wasn't hurting before,' Hong said, accusingly.

'Oh, shut up,' Judy said. 'You don't know.'

'He's right,' I blubbed. 'It wasn't hurting before. It's just started to hurt, and it's getting worse and worse.'

My brother looked as if he still didn't believe me so I said, 'Ooooah,' and grabbed my nose.

'There,' Judy said, holding me and looking accusingly at Hong. 'There, it's hurting like anything. You can tell.'

'Ooooah,' I said.

Judy got me to lie down on her bed and pulled down the blind. 'You try to sleep,' she said. 'Mum will be back soon. Or should I go and get Dad?'

'No,' I said. 'I'll be all right. Don't worry Dad.'

They left me in the darkened room. I lay there for a while,

then picked up a book, which I had to hold near the window to read properly.

Suddenly I sensed Hong was outside watching me under the blind. I dropped the book and let out an oooah and he disappeared.

When Mum came home things began to move. First she came in and asked me a lot of questions, looked up my nose, but said she could see nothing and told me not to breathe in through my nose as it could be dangerous. Then Dad came and put his hand, that felt like Mum's pot scrubber, on my forehead and said, 'Poor old chap,' and smiled. He told me he was going out to catch Star, and Mum would take me in to the doctor's.

Then I began to feel terribly sorry for myself. I wished I hadn't put on such an act about it hurting, because it wasn't, and I would have liked to tell everyone. But I couldn't go back on that now. It was all Judy's fault. If she had shown a little sympathy in the first place it would have been different.

We got dressed up and went out into the rain. Dad had found an old canvas to wrap over our backs and legs. 'Are you sure you won't let me take him, Ame?' my father said, as we were about to leave. 'The milking can wait.'

'Rubbish!' Mum said and smiled. 'It'll blow away the cob-webs.' It was almost as if she enjoyed the idea of going out in the pouring rain. Dad grinned. We left him with a bag over his shoulders, on his way back to the cowshed.

We had seven miles to go and old Star, who was lazy on the best of days, had no liking for the rain that belted down on us, and less for the buckle on the reins' end that Mum kept slapping him with, until he got the idea that we were in a hurry.

Half-way up the second paddock Mum's umbrella turned inside out. She closed it up and threw it in the back of the cart.

Next door, Mr Ernie Bassett was standing, tall, and bent

78

like the curly pipe he always held in his gums, in the doorway of the barn, watching.

Miss Fanny and Miss Bea were in their garden in big hats
and raincoats chasing several sheep which had probably got
through the fence. They waved and Mum waved back and
said to me, 'You see, we all have our little troubles. It'd be a
dull old world without troubles.'

All the neighbours seemed to see us: faces at windows
moving behind lace curtains, black figures, still for a
moment, like stumps in paddocks. Mr Ernie Norton Smith
crossed the road in front of us with his twelve-bore and three
hounds. He waved to us with his gun barrel, and made me
think of Frank and Loch and all the rabbits we could have
got if only Judy hadn't fallen in the hole.

Then Mum was laughing. I looked up at her, her face
streaming with rain. 'I was just thinking,' she said, 'the
whole district will be trying to work out why Mrs Roberts
and her little boy should be going anywhere on a day like
this. They always think of the worst. They always do in the
country. They'll have you with acute appendicitis, or snake
bite, but never, never a pea up your nose. I'll wager someone
will be down before we get home to ask your father.'

I laughed too. It made me feel better, but I was still
puzzled how Mum could be in such a good humour and not
be angry with me.

At the bridge the river was lapping over the decking and
Star was ready to stop or shy away but Mum was ready for
him. She slashed him with the whip, which she hardly ever
used, and we were across and belting along the metal road
before he knew.

It could have been the jerk as Star bounded forward, but
suddenly I felt the pea was loose in my nostril. I waited until
Mum was engrossed looking at acres of water on the flats
where the two rivers met. I could feel it all right. Carefully I
hooked a fingernail under it, eased it out and held it tight in

the palm of my hand.

Halfway up the big hill before the main road Mum gave Star a spell. Even there, with the rain slashing at our faces and bouncing in a white crust off the horse's back, Mum was able to point out Medwin's white rooster under a bush, feathers stuck to its back, and tail dragging, and say how sad it looked. That rooster sad!

We reached the top of the hill and Mum gave the reins a flick. 'I'm so grateful Star is freshly shod,' Mum said, and smiled at me through the rain. 'You see, things are never so bad they could not be worse. All sorts of things can happen. You could have had a pea up each of your nostrils, which would have been twice as bad.'

I was pleased it was raining then, because I knew the tears were running down my cheeks, but washed off so thoroughly I couldn't even taste the salt. The horse clopped. The water flew off the iron wheels. In my hand, held, like I would hold a favourite marble, was the cause of all the trouble, the pea.

'It won't be long now,' my mother said. 'Just down the main street and then along to Doctor's.'

There were only a few people in the street, but no-one took much notice of us except a man in a white apron standing at the door of the grocer's shop. He waved and my mother nodded so that the water sprayed off the rim of her hat.

I pressed closer to her and she took her hand out from under the canvas and put it around my shoulders. 'It won't be long now,' she said.

Suddenly I struggled forward in a mock sneeze and straightened up. I opened my palm and looked up at Mum.

She stopped the horse and looked at the wet pea lying in the palm of my hand.

She threw back her head and laughed.

And I laughed too.

Still laughing, she slashed the startled horse with the reins and swung around on the road, pulling hard on the bit.

'Come on, you stupid beast,' she said, 'and hurry or we'll never get across the bridge.'

FRIDAY NIGHT SHOPPING

Suddenly I realized there was a man approaching out of the darkness from the rear of the shop, on the other side of the counter. Not by the sound, his approach was quite silent. (I wondered was he wearing socks or were his feet bare.) It was, at first, the blur of a face, then yellow-brown, smiling. A short man, no taller than me.

'You like somesinks?'

It was a pleasant voice, clipped and sing-song. It could even have been the same Chinaman who came regularly to our place in his covered wagon to buy rabbit skins. Perhaps he recognized me, but then he had the advantage, because I knew that all white Australians looked different whereas Chinamen were as alike as a mob of sheep.

'You like somesinks?' he repeated.

His thin fingers rested on the edge of the counter, curled as if he were about to play a chord.

'Crackers, please,' I said. 'Six pennyworth.'

'Crackers. Six pennies.'

He took down a long shallow box and selected a number of different crackers and laid them on the counter. 'You like?'

I selected a flowerpot, two double bangers, a jumping jack. 'And how many tom thumbs?' He pushed over a few small ones on to my pile. 'No more?' He smiled, showing his

82

yellow teeth. 'You good boy, I give extra.' He pushed over a few more. 'Orlite!'

I nodded. He wrapped them in brown paper. I reached out to take them but his hand still rested on the parcel; a small, brown, sinewy hand.

'Six pennies?' He was waiting.

I had the sixpence in my hand ready and gave it to him. The rest of my money, a threepence, two pennies and two halfpennies, everything I had in my pocket, I scooped up and held in my open palm. I looked around to see if anyone was coming in, then leaned over the counter. It was what I had come for. 'Cigarettes,' I whispered. 'One packet of Standard.'

He looked too at the door and, magically, the packet was in his hand. 'Take. Quick. Pocket.'

I snatched it, and thrust it down my front, inside my shirt.

He was smiling again. 'You good boy!'

I looked around when I heard footsteps. At the doorway, Mick Kelleher, a big, red-faced police constable stood, his eyes probably adjusting to the light. 'You too poor to put a light in your shop, Willie?'

'Willie too poor. Willie see enough.' The Chinaman was smiling broadly.

I let the money in my hand clatter on the counter, snatched up the brown paper parcel and hurried for the door.

The constable put out his hand. 'Just a minute, young fulla! Let's have a look at that parcel, if you don't mind.'

I went with him back to the counter. Willie was still smiling while the constable pulled off the piece of string and undid the parcel.

'Crackers, eh! You going to keep them for Empire Day?'

'No. We've got a bonfire. We're going to light it on Frank's birthday.'

'Frank's birthday, eh. Frank who?'

'Roberts. Frank is my brother.'

83

'You one of old Kay's boys, out at Flowerdale?'

'Yes.' Old Kay – why did they all –

'Well, you tell young Frank if I catch him in Wynyard without a proper exhaust on that motorbike of his I'll kick his quoit for him, right!' He put his hand out and ruffled my hair. That same hair that I had so carefully oiled and parted, expecially to come in to town with Dad and Loch and Frank; (the first time ever for me, for Friday night shopping).

And then he said it again, looking down at me with a half grin on his face, 'Old Kay, eh. Game little bloke. He used to be captain of the Mersey team. Rove all four quarters. Couldn't stop him, those days. Saw him play in the veteran's football a while back. Well over fifty then, they tell me. Saw him knocked flat on his face in the mud, came up looking like a black fella. Didn't stop him though, pulled the mud out of his eyes an' away he went. Old Kay's boy, eh! What's your name?'

'Bernard.'

'Bernard, eh. Got a nickname?'

I hesitated. Then, 'Scrub,' I said.

'Scrub, eh. Scrub Roberts. Then off you go, Scrub.' I went to run out of the shop, even forgetting the parcel, until he said, 'Don't forget your parcel.' And handed it to me.

He started to walk towards the door with me. 'Righto, Willie,' he said.

'One minute, Boy!' It was Willie.

We both stopped and turned. He had money on the counter.

'You give me tillypence, four pennies. One pennies too much.' He was holding out a penny.

'Go on, Scrub. Never knock back anything Willie gives. It don't happen often.'

I went back to the counter and took the penny. Willie was smiling. He held on to the penny just long enough to make me look up to see the slight, but unmistakeable wink. I knew

I had not made a mistake with the money. Somehow I felt I had scored a victory. Even Mick Kelleher calling Dad Old Kay didn't worry me so much. I could tell he admired him. And Willie. I wondered whether he was the skin buyer. We often chanted off what we thought (had been told by someone, but couldn't guess who) were the names of the four Chinamen, who lived at the back of the shop: Wooey Fungkit, Niang Seepo, Muck Den, Ah Kooee. It may have been all a joke, yet on the other hand could Wooey be really Willie. I decided it didn't matter anyway.

Mick Kelleher was going up the street so I went down. I saw Loch and Frank outside Con O'Neill's shop talking and laughing with some bigger boys I didn't know, so kept going. I had told Dad I would meet him on Hamilton's corner, or at the car.

I stopped outside Cryan's Hotel to listen to the Salvation Army band which was in a circle on the street and a young woman with a bonnet and a smile was holding out a money box and rattling it at all the passers-by. The song the band was playing was the same one the Salvation Army man had tried to teach us some years ago at the Boar Harbour School. I tried to remember the words, but couldn't. It was something about a house or a mansion with many doors and you go in the front door and I'll go in the back. But, think as I tried, it wouldn't come back to me. Of course I was only six at the time and I had only heard it once.

I stood there on the side looking at the ring of musicians, all with an instrument; some brass, some silver, and two others with clicker things they beat time with; and a man with a drum. A few of them were not in uniform, and they all looked ordinary sort of people: one was a man I had seen once down at the wharf, on a fishing boat, when we were going over the river on Arthur Titley's rowing-boat ferry to a picnic with the Lewis's.

Then the music stopped. The girl with the money box

looked at me and smiled. I put my hand over my shirt where the cigarettes were and turned guiltily away.

Dad was not outside Hamilton's.

As I crossed the street to walk down to the car a short, thick-set man walked out on the street and started shouting. I realized he would be one of the gospellers Frank and Loch had told me about. A small knot of people stood on the footpath near him, the men were holding their hats in big, curled, farmer's hands, the women were dressed in dark clothes, their faces, mostly old and wrinkled, were all browned with wind and sun, all serious and tired looking, not like the Salvation Army people who I thought had looked jolly, like their music.

Further down the street several young men were chiacking the preacher. One ran out on the road and yelled, 'Save me, Jesus!' and the others doubled up with laughter. A man in a T Ford honked his horn at the preacher, but the preacher turned his back and went on preaching. The man in the car had to drive around him, which he did, honking and honking, much to the amusement of the onlookers.

I found Dad at the car. He told me not to go away as he only had to pick up his boots from Mr Evans the boot repairer. Loch and Frank, he told me, would be waiting to be picked up at the Central Hall. 'I shan't be long,' he said.

I sat in the car idly watching people moving up and down the street. Most of the shops were on the other side, but a few shoppers were still going in or out of Baker's Hardware.

The Salvation Army band must have moved up to the Mount Lyell Hotel because they had started playing again but sounded much farther away now. The preacher was still shouting out to anyone who would listen. I turned around to kneel on the seat, and, folding my arms over the back rest, I stared out the back window. The group of young men had gone. I saw them crossing the street further up and watched them go into Cryan's.

I felt the packet of cigarettes sticking into my stomach and suddenly wished I hadn't bought it. Cocky Bassett and I had tried smoking tea-tree bark and stringy-bark from the gum trees around home, in Norton-Smith's creek. We had each taken slithers off our fathers' Victory pipe tobacco and rolled that up in squares of newspaper. Once I had smoked a bit of a cigar someone had given Dad. Every time I had tried smoking I had finished up feeling sick in the stomach. After the cigar I had become quite giddy and had to sit with my head in my hands in the rushes, where I had hidden until I felt better.

I had heard of so many of the school boys who had bought cigarettes from the Chinaman that I wanted to get some. But now that I had done it, I didn't want them. I would happily have given them away. How could I keep them hidden from the rest of the family? When would I smoke them? I could give them to Cocky, but he probably wouldn't want them either.

Idly I watched an old man coming down the street. As he passed I noticed he was muttering. I could see his lips moving. His clothes were ragged, but clean. He shoulders were hunched forwards as if he were carrying a big weight on the back of his neck.

I waited until he had passed then took the packet out of my shirt and hurried after him. I touched him on the arm. 'Did you lose these,' I said.

He looked at me, then the packet in my hand. He was chewing his bottom lip. 'I don't smoke tailor-mades. Only roll me own. Can't be mine.'

'Take them,' I said. 'I don't know whose they are.'

He was frowning and chewing again at his lip. 'Go on,' I said.

He reached out a hand. I noticed that his fourth finger was missing and the first and second were brown from nicotine. 'Thanks, Son,' he said.

NINE BEAN ROWS

'The Curfew tolls the Knell of parting Day,
The lowing Herd winds slowly o'er the Lea,
The Plowman homeward plods his weary Way,
And leaves the World to Darkness and to me.'
'– I always get stuck there!'
'Now fades the glimmering Landscape on the Sight –'
'Yes, now I've got it.'

Loch and Mum were at it again. I could hear them from
the back garden where Hong and I were skinning rabbits
which we had shot up on King's. It all started when Loch
came up from turning the cows onto the flats after the evening milking. He was telling Mum how he had looked up to
see Tas Ridge going home with the horses after ploughing
one of his paddocks over the river, hence Gray's Elegy.

We weren't saying anything, because, I was listening to
Loch and Mum, and Hong was concentrating on his job. We
had three each to skin and Hong was going flat out trying to
finish his before I finished mine. I was pretty fast skinning
but I suddenly realized he had his foot on the back legs of his
second one and was pulling the skin up over its head. I was
behind. Well behind.

I put on a spurt but still finished second. We slit the bellies
from the tails up to the ribs and one at a time bent the
carcases backwards, holding the four legs in one hand, and

flipped the guts out, like you'd crack a whip, in one clean throw, to land yards away under the elder trees. We pegged out the skins on the wires, tied the legs and did another count on the total number we had lined up ready to sell to the Chinaman.

We picked out the three best carcases for Mum to take to Wynyard; kept the back ends of two young bucks and gave the rest to the dogs. They had quite a feast after we had given two cats a head each.

Mum took the ones she wanted, to soak in a basin of salt water overnight.

After Dad bought the car, Mum said she wasn't interested in learning to drive, which meant that every CWA day, once a month, and at least one other day in the month Dad had to get dressed up to take Mum in shopping. Mum used to say that it did Dad good to get out, but he never looked very excited, and always tried to make some excuse why he couldn't go, but in the finish he always went.

I think he quite enjoyed it once he got going. Mum always said he did anyway.

Mum rarely went to town without taking something from the vegie garden, or potatoes, or rabbits, or a pot of jam of some sort, to give to somebody. And mostly now one or both of the Miss Norton-Smiths were picked up on the way.

I knew one of the rabbits was going to be for Mr Bethune because he was very fond of rabbit and he had been sick, which, I guessed, meant that he had been drinking too much. Once I heard that someone in Burnie had rung Doctor Smellie to say that they had seen JW drunk and sitting on the footpath with his feet in the gutter, and his head in his hands. The picture stuck in my mind after that. I lay awake for a while the night after I heard it, wishing I could lead him off to where nobody would see him.

Because the Smellies were friends of his, Doc Smellie had taken him home to his place to care for him.

Some of the 'better' people of Wynyard wanted to get rid of JW because, they said, he was 'a bad influence'.

It was because he respected and helped people in spite of their weaknesses and infirmities (sometimes, I thought, because of them) that I loved him; that he gave me hope and courage. (The strong and the perfect always left me feeling deficient and inadequate.)

The last time Mum had been to the rectory, she saw the housekeeper, Miss Wilson, who would never hear a word against JW, no matter what.

Miss Wilson had told her how it had taken her months to convince him that he must buy himself some new boots because his others were beyond repair. He had worn the new ones for several weeks, then one day she noticed he was wearing the old ones again. On questioning, he told her the old ones were more comfortable, but eventually admitted he had given the new ones away to some person who he said needed them more than he did. Miss Wilson had been angry and scolded him and he had smiled and said, 'I had two pairs of boots and gave away those which were less comfortable. Is that a sin?'

Mum was taking another rabbit and some potatoes to a very poor family: a man, who worked when and wherever he could get a job, a woman, whom Mum described as 'a poor, miserable creature, who had had all ambition squeezed out of her', and three children who were thin and dressed in rags.

Mum always came back from their place feeling depressed. The last time she had found the mother had the youngest home from school, a victim of the diptheria epidemic which was sweeping through the Wynyard School in May. She had asked to see the child and had been taken through into a bedroom where the mother and father obviously slept. The scrim and paper had come away from the paling ceiling and had bellied down to within a few feet of the bed where the child lay, almost hidden in a mess of blankets.

When she returned home, she saw Loch in the garden and strings pulled tight in rows on a freshly planted bed. She walked down to him.

'What have you planted?'

'Beans.'

'Beans! Good.' She was still thinking of the jungle of grass and thistles which surrounded the cottage where the child lay under the tired ceiling. 'Yes. That's good. "Nine bean rows will I have there . . ."'

'A hive for the honey bee . . .'

'And I shall have some peace there . . .' Self-accusation – as if she were to blame.

'You missed a line,' Loch said, not looking up.

'Yes, I know.' And turned with her few parcels for the house. She heard him muttering, 'And live alone in the bee-loud glade.'

THERE'S A WIND ON THE HEATH, BROTHER

Mum said, 'For the next few nights I'm going to read from the book of Ecclesiastes.'

I knew by the way Dad sat back in his armchair, puffing away at his old pipe, (which would soon need cleaning out again – there was barely room for him to get any tobacco into the bowl, let alone his little finger to pack it) that he was going to enjoy this particular reading.

Dad had probably heard it plenty of times seeing that his father had been a C of E minister, and his grandfather, too.

A lot of it I couldn't understand, but as Mum said, you need to read it over and over. It made me feel depressed, '– all is vanity and vexation of spirit,' and, 'For in much wisdom is much grief: and he that increaseth knowledge increaseth sorrow.' What was the use of trying to learn, trying to understand about things?

'To everything there is a season, and a time to every purpose under the heaven . . . A time to be born and a time to die . . . A time to weep and a time to laugh . . . A time to love and a time to hate . . . A time to keep silence and a time to speak . . . God giveth to a man that is good in his sight, wisdom and knowledge and joy . . .'

It was all jumble and confusion. Well, not all, there was sense in: 'All the rivers run into the sea; yet the sea is not full; unto the place from which the rivers come, thither they return again.' And things like, 'The sun rises and the sun goes down' and, 'The wind blows sometimes from the north and sometimes from the south', and, 'One generation dies and another is born, but the earth is always there.'

But that everything was planned! Was all the work Mum and Dad were doing a waste of time?

'There, so much for that!' Mum said. Then Dad startled me by saying, 'Beautiful.' Just that single word: Beautiful. They smiled at each other, a private, secret, understanding smile. Then Mum said, 'Now I shall read a little of a book written by a man who died when I was one year old, a man called George Borrow, the book is called *Lavengro*. It's a very long book, probably too long to read out, but if we like it I'll read more.'

We did like it. Mum did read more. A lot more. But this time she read only the twenty-fifth chapter which tied in with the Bible reading.

'Lavengro (the Romany word for philologist given Borrow by the Gypsies) is passionately interested in languages, in people, in travelling. He is obsessed by his failure to find a satisfactory answer to the perennial problem: What is Truth?'

I became immediately interested. 'In what did I not doubt!' he said. 'For what was I born? Are not all things born to be forgotten? That's incomprehensible, yet is it not so? Those butterflies fall and are forgotten. In what is man better than a butterfly?'

If God made me, then who made God? the simplest of all age-old questions, yet one which had concerned me in meditative moments, even, I think, before I started going to school. And here at last was a man with the same doubts who seemed to be leading me towards a new understanding. I had had the feeling that children were supposed never to be concerned with problems of the mind; that all required was patience: wisdom came with age, and with wisdom all questions were answered. Yet here was Lavengro, intelligent, wise, searching for the answer: What is Truth?

'Now this last piece,' my mother said, 'has been described as the most beautiful piece in literature. Mr Petulengro is Lavengro's Gypsy friend.'

'What is your opinion of death, Mr Petulengro?' said I, as I sat down beside him.

'My opinion of death, brother, is much the same as that in the old song of Pharaoh, which I have heard my grandam sing . . . When a man dies he is cast into the earth, and his wife and child sorrow over him. If he has neither wife nor child, then his father and mother, I suppose; and if he is quite alone in the world, why, then, he is cast onto the earth, and there is an end of the matter.'

'And do you think that is the end of man?'

'There's an end of him, brother, more's the pity.'

'Why do you say so?'

'Life is sweet, brother.'

'Do you think so?'

'Think so! There's night and day, brother, both sweet things; sun, moon and stars, brother, all sweet things; there's likewise a wind on the heath. Life is very sweet, brother; who would wish to die?'

'I would wish to die.'

'You talk like a Gorgio – which is the same as talking like a fool. Were you a Romany Chal, you would talk wiser. Wish to die, indeed! A Romany Chal would wish to live for ever!'

'In sickness, Jasper?'

'There's the sun and stars, brother.'

'In blindness, Jasper?'

'There's the wind on the heath, brother; if I could only feel that, I would live for ever. Dosta, now we'll go to the tents and put on the gloves; and I'll try to make you feel what a sweet thing it is to be alive, brother!

'Now,' Mum said, shutting the book. 'Bedtime.'
'Can we have more, tomorrow?'
'You may!' And smiled.

At the River

They didn't go there often as they didn't want to fish it out but it was still their favourite fishing hole. Bern and Henry lay in the shade of the willows on the trunks which jutted out over the river.

The trunks were bigger round than the boys' bodies and almost horizontal at the base. The bark was not a smooth green like the young branches, but dark brown and furrowed like old Mrs Higson's face and neck. Not really like that, Bern thought; her wrinkles were not as deep and there were a lot more of them.

He looked over at Henry who was stretched out on his tree. He was holding his hand flat, out from his eyes, peering down into the black water. 'There's one there,' he said. 'He keeps coming up for a sniff, but goes away again.' He didn't even look at Bern when he spoke. Bern knew he would keep his eye on the fish and with his other hand move the line slowly over to tempt the fish to grab the worm.

Bern noticed the red beard clinging to the bottom of Henry's tree, barely moving in the still water. Mr Higson had a beard something that colour. He was old too; like his wife. You couldn't see his face and neck but you could tell by the backs of his hands; when he laid them out flat they looked like Mrs Webster's relief map of Tasmania at school, showing all the rivers and creeks and mountains, and there were brown patches like Charlie Byard's freckles, only twice as big, reaching up to his elbows. Bern thought that the Higsons must be the oldest people in the world.

Henry was winding his line around the stub of stick. They never used dogwood rods when they were fishing in dead holes; they only got in the way. 'He took my bait,' Henry said. When he stood up Bern noticed the marks on his body and legs where the bark had dug into his bare flesh leaving white weals like old scars that seemed to fade as he watched.

Henry walked back along the trunk onto a piece of drift-wood not as wide as his feet. It rested, one end on the bank, the other stuck in the fork of the tree. Absently Bern watched his brother walk along the rickety spar, clinging to it with his toes. Funny how some kids, particularly town kids, had no sense of balance; but then town kids didn't have post and rail fences to practise walking on. Bern and Henry had started off by walking on the railway lines, until they could walk a mile without falling off, even jumping from one rail to the other every time they passed a telephone pole.

Henry dug a worm out of the bait tin and threaded it onto the hook so that it was free to waggle a bit.

'Bring us one down,' Bern said. 'Mine is about dead.'

He took the worm off the hook and threw it far out over the river. It landed with barely a dimple on the water, which was shining as if someone were holding a mirror flat on its surface; almost blinding when you looked at it.

Two swallows were sporting backwards and forwards, skimming the water and leaving two trails, which closed over almost immediately. 'They're the ones nesting under the railway bridge. They had three eggs yesterday.' Henry was watching them too. 'I wonder why they touch the water like that. You'd think they might dive just a bit too deep.' But they never did, of course. After all any bird which can pick up insects at the speed they travel . . . He liked watch-ing them soar and swoop and skim the grass, and the drain from the cowshed after they had washed down. And always so friendly; unafraid to come onto their nest when people were about.

He was still holding the worm which Henry had given him. It kept wriggling, trying to escape between his fingers, so he had to shake it back into his palm. He took it at last and slid the barb of the hook into its body just below the head and pushed it on until the entire hook was covered. He had often noticed, whenever he threaded a worm onto his hook, he found he had to grind his teeth. He knew he was soft.

'They don't feel nothin',' one of the big boys at school had said. But why, if they didn't, did they twist and squirm like they did? This kid had kicked over a lump of horse manure. As soon as the light hit it the worm underneath dived for its burrow but the kid grabbed it and stretched it almost to breaking before it flipped out of its hole. He had thrown it on to the ground and crunched it into a pulp with his boot. 'That'll learn yer to be a worm,' the kid had said.

Some of the others had laughed.

When Bern went home he asked his father if worms could feel anything. His father got a book off the shelf and turned the pages. 'Here's a whole book on earth worms,' he said. 'A man called Darwin wrote it – spent years of studying the creatures – interesting, interesting – real friend of the farmer.' But he couldn't see quickly anything about their sensitivity to pain. 'You should read it.' Afterwards when Bern asked his mother she said she thought they would feel pain like any other living creature, but probably not as much as people.

Bern let the line fall slowly into the water. He leaned over the trunk, shading the water so that he could see to the bottom. A few willow leaves shone yellow on the river bottom. He eased the line over near a large submerged log, under which the fish lived. He could see the tail of one waving slowly sideways. He dropped the line until the sinker rested on the bottom and the worm, still wriggling, was a few inches from the log. The tail disappeared and a small black-fish darted out and snapped off a piece of the worm. He jerked the line to frighten away the fish. He wasn't interested in those little ones. He reset the line, sat up and curled the line around his big toe. He looked across at his brother who was on his tummy, slowly easing his line through the water. 'I got a bite,' Bern said. 'It was only a brat.'

'There's a good one here,' Henry said, 'about half a pound. He's nearly taken it a few times.' He was almost whispering, as if the fish might hear and duck back under cover of the log. Then suddenly he jerked the line and stood up. He had hooked him through the side of his mouth; a nice fish, shiny black and flapping. He ran up the spar on the bank and threw the fish onto the paddock. He broke off a small willow branch and with his sheath knife cut a longer main stem to hold it by and sharpened a shorter branch which he would stick through the gill and out of the fish's mouth, after cracking it on the back of the head with a knife handle.

Bern leaned his back against the trunk where it curved up vertically. He could go to sleep there easily enough. The day was warm and still; pleasant under the willows, above the running water, and no flies there in the shade. It was one of those rare November days when the whole world slept. Except for the swallows, even the birds were still; even the blue wrens, Henry's favourites: there must be hundreds of them along the river. Or thousands.

Henry was back on his trunk again. Bern watched him setting the line, exactly as he wanted it. He always did things well; always that bit better than Bern, (who was two years older): setting traps, shooting rabbits, fishing, diving, cricket; even at school he had caught up a year. But Bern didn't mind. They were the best of friends; always had been; always would be, probably.

The red beard of the willow caught his eye, waving slightly in the current. He thought again of Mr Higson. Probably for ever afterwards he would think of Mr Higson whenever he saw a willow tree with those red hairy water roots waving; or Mrs when he saw the crinkled bark; but not so much.

'How old do you think the Higsons are?' Bern asked.

'The Higsons!' Henry gave a half laugh. Bern was often coming out with something like that, nothing to do with fishing. 'Don't know. About ninety. Why?'

'Just wondering.'

'Will we have a swim before we go back?'

'Yeah, let's.' Bern unwound the line from his toe and tugged. 'I think I'm snagged.' But it wasn't a snag. It was an eel; a long, thick, slimy eel that had swallowed the line almost up to where the lead sinker was attached.

'Gee, it's thick,' Henry was saying. Bern grinned. 'And long.' He was thinking about thick chunks of eel meat sizzling in the frying pan for breakfast in the morning.

But there was a lot to do first, before that happened: to unknot the line that the eel had somehow twisted itself around with its sinuous threshings, to hold the thing, so slippery and slimy, and so ready to wind itself around your leg or arm, or to slap your face, to kill it, to skin it. Loch was a champion at that – nail its tail to a post, rub his hands and the skin with dry dirt or sand and pull off in one piece, like a sock.

Although the day was hot and cloudless, the water was cold when they dived in. They were perfectly at home in the dark water. They knew, in this stretch of river, where the snags and the submerged logs were. They loved to show off in front of the neighbours' kids, diving down to bring up handfuls of gravel or a black slimy stick that had probably been stuck in the river bed for years. Funny how hardly any of the school kids knew how to swim. If someone dropped anything into the river: 'Hey, one of them Robertses'll get it out for yer.' They had all learned not long after they could walk; by their dad walking in front of them down that shallow stretch below the railway bridge holding them up, only by two fingers under their chin, while they threshed and kicked and spluttered.

But today there were just the two of them. Bern, breast-stroking and Henry, with his long, arm-thrusting dog-paddle. And then the two of them floating down with the current on their backs, hands down near their sides, flat like fins, moving gently backwards and forwards. They could float for ages like this, looking up at the sky, head back but keeping an eye on the snags and branches, steering out into the current; down under the railway bridge, drifting past the piles like two logs: or stopping, holding on to them and clambering up on to the cross beams to wait for the train that roared louder and louder as it came onto the bridge, and gravel dropping down on them and plopping into the water. Then they always had that scary feeling. But Bern never admitted it because his younger brother never did. But on those occasions, when the train had gone, they would stand on the cross beam and piss into the water. And laugh.

But today they didn't float far. The water was too cold. They swam out on to the bank on Ridge's side, up the little gravel beach and onto the long grass where cows raised their heads to stare at these two crazy animals, skinny and white, whooping and wind-milling across the paddock and back. Henry started it by scooping up a handful of cowshit and Bern's white bum was painted with a map of Tasmania, and then his legs, and both of them splattered, and rolling, and wrestling, and the cows even walking closer to watch, with tails swishing and necks craned forwards, ready at a moment's notice to fly, just in case these strange animals did suddenly turn into savage dogs.

When they had washed themselves and each other and hurried, shivering, to lie on the warm gravel with the sun beating down on them, Bern thought of the cows and how inquisitive they were and how, for all their size, they were gentle and scared, except when they had a calf, then they would become bellowing, angry maniacs if a dog came too near.

And thinking of dogs Bern was reminded of the story about old Mr Ridge, how the insurance man walked down on to the flats to find him rounding up the cows and asked him, 'Are you Mr Ridge?' and Mr Ridge had looked at the insurance man and spoke slowly, like he did, 'No, son, that's Mr Ridge sittin' up there on that bank lookin' at me. I'm just his flamin' dog.' Except Mr Ridge didn't say 'flaming' he was supposed to have said that other word 'fucking' which neither Bern nor Henry dared say out loud.

'I was just thinking about that story of Mr Ridge and his dog,' Bern said.

'Which one?'

'With the insurance man.'

'That! But what about the other one, how he got sick of the old dog not going for the cows so he told him – "You're going to go today, dog," – and put him under his arm and carried him all the way down to the flat and home again. I reckon he must have got covered with fleas.'

They both laughed and, just as if one of them had suggested it, they both dived in to have one more quick swim before going home.

'Hey!' Henry's sharp eyes spied it. Normally it would have been below the water level but with the dry summer – 'Would that be a platypus burrow?' They turned together like dogs after a native hen, across the current, and clung to the bank.

They could see the worn and padded entrance. Their dad had told them there'd be a burrow about there somewhere. There was always at least one platypus swimming about there in the early morning or late afternoon. 'They dig a burrow,' he had said, 'about six or eight yards long below water level.'

'Perhaps, because the river is so low – '

Excited by their find, they hurried back to dress and to collect the fish and the eel.

They had seen their first platypus burrow. That was really something to tell them at home.

Bern looked up at the sky. He was surprised to see how low the sun was. It was still warm but as he watched a small wind puckered the face of the water. If they hid for a while the platypuses would be out feeding.

They turned when they heard the pony trap on the track over the river. It was old Mr Fist who had treated one of their father's cows for milk fever a few weeks before by pumping up the udder with a bike pump. But the cow had later died. He saw them and waved. His long beard was waving and jiggling with the movement of the trap.

'I suppose he would be about ninety,' Bern said.

'Or a hundred!' said Henry.

VOICES AND FACES

You could hear every word, probably because we knew what the words should be. That would help. Mrs Kelv Snare was singing.

> 'Now the day is over,
> Night is drawing nigh,
> Shadows of the evening
> Steal across the sky.'

Mrs Kelv often sang. Mostly in the evenings. Mostly hymns.

I would have been either six or seven on this particular occasion, because it was only in those years that I attended Boat Harbour State School.

I remember coming down Snare's lane. I was walking behind the others with Bunny King at the time, when I noticed a single sheet and a blanket on the line at home. I hoped no one else would notice them and say, 'Who peed their bed last night?' Nobody did. But I wished Mum wouldn't hang them there, so they could be seen. Anyone going to State School and still peeing their bed, if only occasionally, was a bit of a joke. And I had enough to contend with.

The others went down to the river bank below the railway bridge. Jude and I stopped for a while on the bridge watching them roll stones down the bank into the water, then walked slowly along the line, kicking at the white gravel on the sleepers.

Sometimes Mum would walk a bit of the way to meet us. We saw her gathering a few dry ferns by the white gates at the crossing and ran to meet her.

'Here,' she said, 'I've brought a few biscuits. Where are the boys?'

'They are playing with the Kings back at the Big Bridge.' (There were three bridges: Little, Middle and Big, joined by an embankment which crossed our flats and the Flowerdale River.)

I took Mum's free hand and we walked on slowly towards the house. We were just going through the gate into the calf paddock when Mrs Kelv started singing. We stopped and looked up at Snare's house about a mile away up on the side of the hill.

Out by the clothes line in the yard I could see her standing. Quite still. 'She must be proud of her voice,' I said. 'She often sings out in the yard.'

'Perhaps she just feels good,' Mum said. 'You know, she has quite a good voice. Certainly a strong one, even with this north westerly blowing.'

> 'Now the darkness gathers,
> Stars begin to peep,
> Birds, and beasts and flowers,
> Soon will be asleep.'

'She's a little premature.' Mum smiled. 'Strange, how clear it is. It's coming straight down the gully. Probably bouncing off Brandy Creek.'

'Does sound bounce off water?'

'I'm not sure. That's something you can ask Mr Burns at school tomorrow. Or perhaps your father may know. Ask him.'

'Dad's sure to know,' I said. 'He'd know a lot more than Mr Burns.' I still hadn't forgiven Mr Burns for cutting my finger open with a split cane.

Ivan King did have a good voice. A rich baritone, so Dad said. And he certainly enjoyed singing. Ivan, (or Ring, as he was called) was still going to school but his voice had broken and he was evidently as fascinated with the new sound as I was.

The Kings lived over the river at the end of Snare's Lane. How they got their nicknames I never knew. I did know the first six boys in the family by their various names: Ivan was Ring, Douglas – Digger, Maurice – Squit, Ross – Dodger, Egbert – Bunny and Maxwell – Shunter. They were all good cricketers. Only Ivan could sing well.

> 'There's a Cross, there's a Cross
> Where old Feathers lost his horse.'

Feathers Watts had been ambushed by some naughty schoolboys at the rail crossing and Feathers had been left behind when his horse bolted. The song based on a Salvation Army tune could sometimes be heard by a chorus led by a rich baritone voice over the river.

'How're they hangin'?' It was Les's way of saying Hullo or Good-day through cupped hands from wherever he was on the hill, half a mile away over the river. It always brought a smile to our faces and a more publically acceptable reply like 'What are yer doin'?' or 'How are yer goin'?' or in Loch's case, a loud prolonged whistle blown through the knuckles of his thumbs into the chamber of two hands held tightly cupped, or released to alter the note. (Something I spent hours trying to master, but never did.)

I could imagine the Misses Norton Smith, who were also within earshot, stopping for a moment, straightening up from one of their constant and absorbing tasks in their beautiful garden at Amberley, to stare up to the slopes from where the voice came; perhaps shaking heads in disapproval. Perhaps even enjoying it as a voice of the valley.

I had watched Les sometimes cutting wood and never failed to be, at first puzzled, then, after Dad explained (that it normally takes sound about a second to travel eleven hundred feet) intrigued by the way the sound of the axe hitting the log came when the axe was high in the air.

> Auntie Mary had a canary
> Up the leg of her drawers.
> Said Auntie Mary to the canary,
> 'Go easy with those claws.'

We made sure we never sang it within earshot of Aunt Mary.

Sometimes Cocky called Auntie Mary, Auntie Pol. We always made sure we called her Miss Bassett.

Except on Sundays, she always seemed to be wearing a bag apron, which hung almost down to her boots. It was used to gather pinecones and gum bark and sticks; and afforded an ideal excuse for her to be down at the road under the pine trees to check out any passer-by, or any strange vehicle, or to go through the mail (which was put by one or other of the neighbours in a community box on the cream stand) to see who was getting letters and, by their postmark, where they had come from.

Cocky and Bowler and Hong and I were in Bassett's big barn one day. We had come in the back way so Auntie Mary wouldn't see us, but she must have been snooping around to see where we were.

She came sneaking through the door to find us in the old cart (which I had never seen on the road – they didn't even own a cart horse). She was holding a swishy gum stick and yelled at Cocky, because he was the oldest, 'I'll skin you,

Cocky. Get out of that cart!'

I asked Cocky afterwards if she had often hit him, and Cocky said, 'She's never hit none of us. She's all bluff.'

We added Auntie Mary's 'I'll skin you, Cocky' to our repertoire of sayings for local use.

I said to Mum one day, 'I feel sorry for Miss Bassett.' And Mum said, 'I feel sorrier for Mrs Bassett. Poor Mabel has had her sister-in-law and her brother-in-law living with her all her married life.'

I wasn't sure why that would be so bad. I always liked any of our relations to come to stay with us.

J. W. was how we referred to John Walter Bethune M.A. Cantab.

When I was at Flowerdale School in 1928 he was asked to resign his position as Headmaster of the Launceston Church Grammar School.

I knew little about the man apart from knowing my parents had a very high opinion of him and were thrilled to know he was to be the new vicar of the Anglican Church in Wynyard. There were whispered stories that he was an alcoholic, but that was something we didn't discuss at home.

As I learned to know him I grew to love him. He gave us a cricket bat because he found a number of us playing cricket in a paddock at Moorleah with a rough-hewn willow. He would stop to talk with any of us on the road. He seemed to ferret out poor people to help. He tousled my hair or gave me a playful stripe on the bottom with his stick which he used not as an aid to walking but more as an adornment.

His straight upright walk, his close cropped hair, his ears hugging his head, his direct look and simple, straightforward way of speaking reason and, I think, his sense of drama all made me admire him and for the first time want to go to church at the monthly services at Moorleah.

Moorleah was both a social and a religious occasion. J. W. was low church and couldn't be fussed with any of the trappings which some ministers insisted upon. His main purpose always was to get across to the congregation his philosophy of love, and help, and understanding for the poor, and his hatred for hypocrisy and selfishness.

In one sermon when he was being critical, both of the clergy and the church, he ended with (as Mum put it: 'that delightfully provocative and pugnacious thrust of opinion'), 'It is better for the churches to be closed, than to preach doctrines, contrary to the teachings of Christ.'

We would drive as a family once a month to the hall. The hall where also once a month, but on a Saturday night, six or seven times as many people would gather for the local dance. Always the same few people, with Mrs Scotty Stuart playing the piano, gathering, at first outside, and trooping in together, males to the left, females to the right. Always, that is, until Mum, realizing what was happening, said, 'Today Judith, you and I are going to sit with the men. And we'll see what happens.'

So they did! Much to the wonderment of both sides; a small grin from Dad, and was it another from J. W? She had started something, for next month, without warning, Dad and Mum sat on the ladies side which at first caused some confusion but then was accepted as a game.

'Good God, said God, whose God am I?'

How he shouted out that last line! The utter hypocrisy of the Germans and the English each praying for victory to the one God.

Whose God am I? It stayed with me when we walked down the hill to Stuart's for afternoon tea; when we peeped under the bricks and boards on top of the water tin to find six kittens, drowned, bloated, floating on the top of the water; when the Chinaman came to the farm to buy rabbit skins, and the Persian with his drapery. Whose God am I? says God. Is He really the God of the Germans as well?

I have a memory of old Mrs Norton Smith sitting in her chair in a long black dress, all folds, and a lace cap thing over her hair. It could have been a photo. Mrs Norton Smith was Loch's godmother.

Mr Norton Smith was the manager of the Van Diemen's Land Company before he died. He built the big and beautiful weatherboard house on the property which he called Amberley. When we walked the two miles to the Flowerdale School we passed close by the house which was about halfway.

There was one son, Ernest, who was regarded as being pretty rough. I know we thought he was; but he always had a cheery-rough greeting for us. Mum had a special cup for him with a strainer thing across half of it to keep his whiskers out of it, I supposed.

Once when we were coming home from school we watched Mr Norton Smith (Ernie Norton we called him amongst ourselves) with another man marking lambs. Ernie was splattered with blood and piss and shit over his clothes and face. He stood outside the pen while the man inside caught the lambs, held their legs and turned the lamb upside down on the flat rail on the top of the pen fence. Ernie would slit the purse of all the ram lambs, press the agates out with his fingers until they stood tight and smooth like twin almonds, put his bloody, hairy face down over them and one at a time bite them off and spit each testicle at the dog which sat patiently waiting to snap it up in mid-air. 'Never misses,' Ernie said. 'You watch this.' And: Pthoop! Without moving off its tail, the dog had it. 'Look at the shine on his coat, boy. You want to try one. It'd do things to that hair of yours.' We moved back out of range. 'We call him Scrub,' Lester said, 'because his hair always sticks up.' 'Well, there you are! What about taking a few home to your mum, Scrub, old Kay would like 'em. Lamb's fry they call 'em in Scotland – a delicacy.' Old Kay. It was something I couldn't get used to. The kids at school called him, or sometimes me, Kay. It was bringing my father back to the ordinary. We left Ernie to his cutting rams and tails.

There were stories about Ernie Norton Smith. There was the time when he and Arthur Bassett had a fight in the paddock below Bassett's. Neither of them were fighters but in their manoeuvring fell into a stump hole as wide and deep as a shell crater. 'And there they were like a pair o' big lobsters, grapplin' and wrastlin' with each other while we sat on the rim watchin' until they got tired and clambered out.'

And the time when Ernie's mother died. It was said that Ernie had been partly disinherited because of a family row. As the hearse with his mother inside passed his house on the corner, Ernie walked deliberately across the road in front of it with his dogs and gun to go shooting.

Ernie had three sisters, who were very different from him. They always spoke, dressed and acted with extreme care. They were Mum's only real friends in the district. Miss Dulcie, the youngest, married a Dutch sea captain, Dirk Kuipers, and spent most of her time in strange and exotic cities in other lands. Miss Fanny, the oldest, was the managing sort, direct and manly and had no hesitation in scolding us for throwing pinecones into a pond in their paddock, and making us clean up every one when the water dried up. I think I liked her best of all.

Miss Bea, always friendly and generous, sometimes asked Hong and me in for biscuits and cordial on our way home from school. We were even allowed to lie on a deep carpet in the sitting room and read *Snugglepot and Cuddlepie* or one of the children's books which the sisters had read so many years before. We were almost afraid to turn the pages in case we damaged the old books and spent a lot of time looking at the fine ornaments, and the glass bell clock with the brass pendulum, and the cushions covered with delicately worked designs and so clean and white we couldn't imagine how we could ever sit on them let alone throw them at each other.

Once, Miss Fanny told me, they had found Dad on their verandah. He had staggered there and collapsed. The noise of his falling had made them investigate. 'It was when he was baching, the year before he was married,' she told me. 'He had a very severe attack of influenza. We thought at first he was dead.' I could imagine the care and attention he must have had during the days of his illness, from the mother and the three kind-hearted daughters. I loved them all the more for what they had done. I ran off down the path, possibly in a hurry to tell Mum what I knew when the Airedale, Sousa, (who we never really trusted) thinking I must have done something wrong, flew down the path after me and took a chunk out of the seat of my pants; much to the obvious dismay of Miss Fanny.

It seemed impossible. Only yesterday Charlie had driven down the road on his motorbike. And now he was dead! Charlie Smyth dead!

People mostly died of old age. Occasionally after a long illness. Sometimes babies were born dead. Or the mother died. Sometimes pneumonia or diptheria. Everyone at home was upset when the news came. 'I can't believe it!' Mum said. And Dad said, 'Dear-oh-dear!' I tried to think of other things; I tried playing with the dog; but always I came back to thinking: Charlie is dead. And only Frank's age.

Teddy Deverell was up in the Seven Acre digging potatoes. I had to brand some new sacks and carry them up to Teddy. 'And you might like to pick up a few chats while you're there.' It was not a question. Dad probably thought I would be better doing that than mooning about.

I noticed Teddy had about twenty or thirty yards dug when I arrived; that's six rows wide, three rows thrown into one. Without saying anything I started shaking tops, leaving two rows of red-brown tubers, thousands of them, looking clean and fresh. 'Thanks, Bern,' Teddy said, when I caught up with him. It was his job really; a part of his sixpence a bag.

He jabbed his fork into the ground and we walked back to the beginning of the row, together. Teddy was a good digger. Dad employed him whenever he could. Some diggers were faster but mostly, unlike Teddy, stabbed a lot. Dad made a rule that a digger could take home as many as he could carry on his back in a sugar bag. Teddy always took some but never made a welter of it.

'You know what happened last night, Bern?' Ted said.

I thought immediately that he was talking about Charlie, but he wasn't. He went straight on. 'I was riding along The Plains when I heard a buzzing and turned my head a bit and, do you know what, I had a swarm of bees landed on the sugar bag on me back. Riding that last bit home, I can tell yer, I kept as straight as I could, and all the time wondering what I'd do if they worked up on to me neck.'

'What happened? Did they stay there?'

'Until I got home, they did. I took the bag off as careful as you like, hung it on the fence, then I got a kero box, an' now I've got a hive o' bees in the back garden, and only got one sting.'

'Gee, fancy carrying a hive of bees home on your back!'

Teddy was obviously proud of what he had done. I thought how Dad and Loch had got one not long before. Dad stood on a table with a box on his head and Loch, on tip toes, cut the little branch of the magnolia tree they had settled on, so they flopped into the box, and bees went everywhere. Loch took a dive off the table and straight into a camellia bush. Dad pulled fifteen stings out of his arms after he had turned the box upside down on its stand. But they didn't seem to worry him much, particularly after Mum had rubbed his arms with the blue-bag.

Teddy had a swig out of his bottle of cold tea and went on picking up the markers. While I was filling my chat bag I kept thinking about Charlie. I couldn't get him off my mind. It seemed sort of wrong that the only thing Teddy talked about when he stopped was his bees, yet I knew he had told Dad that morning that he had seen where the accident happened; and how Charlie must have been looking over to see if he could see his girlfriend who lived there by the Deep-creek Bridge, and had let his motor bike slew across the road. The cart shaft, he told Dad, must have got him fair in the neck.

All I could think of was the times I had seen Charlie go up and down the road on his motorbike; how when he and Frank had gone off on their tour of Tassy, (right down to Hobart and the East Coast) how Charlie sat there on his bike, outside our garden fence, with all his gear, his long legs touching the ground, that almost permanent smile on his face, the top button of his shirt done up; just talking away to Mum while he was waiting for Frank to tie his gear on the pillion.

We watched them go up the front paddock, both bikes barking; both Frank and Charlie waving as they disappeared over the hill. 'I do hope they drive carefully,' Mum said. She was probably thinking how Frank said so casually how the bike had skidded sideways on loose metal, going down the Hellyer Gorge road, when he, and Les Margetts on the back, were going up to Les's block at Parrawe. 'It wasn't anything,' Frank had said. 'Les and I laughed – only got a bit of a graze.'

The Smyths were our next-door neighbours. Now Charlie was dead!

'I feel so sorry for them all,' Mum said. 'Especially Vivienne. Somehow, I think it must be harder for a mother.' But I was thinking about Jack, his brother, and the two sisters, Florence and Madge. And I couldn't stop thinking how I would feel if it had been one of my own family.

Shekletons bought Cullen's property. Mrs Shekleton was a sister of Reg Hamilton, who owned 'Grey Crags' at Boat Harbour Beach. I had stayed there several times with Ken. Alex Shekleton was the grandson of a magistrate and pioneer of the district. They had one daughter, Betty, about ten years older than me. The pedigrees were good. While not going so far as to leave a card, (they didn't have one anyway) Mum and Dad called with a small gift and a welcome to the district.

Mrs Shek had always been a pioneer, grubbing rushes, milking cows, knocking down walls and putting up new ones in the house. At Cullen's she built a fence and developed a beautiful flower garden which included grubbing stone and laying a crazy stone path. Their furnishings, trophies of better years, were mostly hidden under sheets in a darkened room.

Mrs Shek was a survivor. And as far as Loch was concerned his survival was due to a large extent to Mrs Shek's tireless nursing over the time he spent in a delirium with pneumonia. He was very ill, needing constant care and Mrs Shek, who had been a nurse, helped Mum out by sitting with him each night.

At her place she had a bench and wash tubs in the garden and kept ready-loaded beside her a twelve bore gun to protect her supply of apples, plums, and berry fruit from birds, particularly the cunning blackbirds; but silver eyes, green parrots and starlings were also discouraged from entering her garden; but not in the paddocks, except the crows, which rarely came near, except to the two pear trees ('which Old Man Cullen had planted on the flat by the river, when Queen Victoria was Empress of India').

Invariably, a few days before the pears were ready to pick, the crows would arrive in a flock to pick at and knock to the ground almost the complete crop. ('But I beat the black brutes. I pick them green.' And she would smile her lovely wide smile.)

She loved wrens, finches, honey-eaters and swallows; but for Mrs Shek, as with all country people, the protection of her fruit was imperative in the battle to survive. Pies, puddings, jams and fresh fruit were generally only available if grown on the place. Rarely did she lose her sense of humour; but once, two swallows nesting on the front verandah caused her to tack a piece of tin beneath the nest to catch their droppings which were plastering the floor; then they insisted on shitting over the edge of the tin. When Mrs Shek discovered their betrayal of trust, in a fit of pique (which she regretted later) she gave birds, nest and the previously unperforated roof both barrels.

Hong and I soon found it was different from when the Cullens were there. We asked Mrs Shek one day, when the mulberries were ripe, whether we could pick a few. She said, 'Of course, boys, come with me.' She marched us off down to the tree and pointed at a mulberry. 'Listen now, that mulberry has strychnine on it for the birds so don't touch that whatever you do. And come! Around here, on this side, here's another with strychnine on it for the birds. Don't touch that either!' She left us then and went back to the house. As soon as she disappeared around the corner Hong and I left in a hurry. We wished we had our own mulberry tree at Currajong. Whether she really had used strychnine for the birds we never found out.

Off the farm Mrs Shek's single-seater Chev with a dickey

seat, poor brakes, if any, (twice she had been through the fence at the bottom of Norton's hill) and capable of extraordinary high speeds, caused anyone already on the road to give her ample room. Dressed in her tweed suit and brown hat, with a touch of rouge and lipstick, Mrs Shek, with her scarf flying, waved a greeting to all and sundry. As Mum said once, 'She's so refreshing; not that I want to travel with her, mind.'

As for Mr Shek! 'For a man to be forced to sell that beautiful old property at Seabrook and take on Cullen's at his age requires courage,' Dad said. (Mr Shek was sixty at the time.)

'And courage for her to go with him, at her age, and to work as she does,' Mum added. (Must support her sex.) 'Of course,' Dad said, 'a fine woman. But,' he added with a smile, 'a little reckless, perhaps?'

Mr Shek was a large man, already bending (with the pressures and constant, never-ending worries of the years), who spoke only when necessary and always in a deep, quiet voice. I had the feeling that no matter what the strength of the head winds he might have to face he would plough on at exactly the same speed. His huge hands seemed to remain permanently curled to fit the extra heavy crowbar he had had especially made.

Because he was slightly deaf, he often didn't hear the dinner bell which Mrs Shek had tied to the branch of the big sycamore. Sometimes when he was working the horses, and he reckoned it would be about dinner time, and the horses stopped suddenly, he would wait to see if either of the horses wanted a piss and if not he would say, 'Giddupp!', drive to the end of the row, unhook, and go back for dinner. 'A man doesn't need ears when he's got horses like Prince and Bruce.'

When the Ernie Norton Smiths had gone, the Davises came to manage Amberley. They lived in the old house at the corner of the road. Mr Davis was of a well-known cricketing family. Reg (Bill, or Buster, as some people called him) was a big man and one day, playing at Boat Harbour, he hit each of the first three balls of Nelson King's over for four and the next for a mighty six which travelled right across the road into Hamilton's yard.

Nelson, who was captain of the side, watched the ball sailing high in the air, muttered something about it being a waste of time bowling to that bloke, walked off the field, put his coat on, sat by the log fence, pulled some lunch from his pocket and sent the twelfth man out to field, while he watched.

Oh, but Mr Davis was a good sport!

Who was responsible for the idea I am too ashamed to say; but on a very wet day when the Davises were not at home and the table drain on the road was running a small creek, someone suggested that the drain could be blocked up, which would mean the water could be diverted to run down the path which led to Davis's back door. Jack and Eric Bassett and Hong and I all helped in the construction of the small dam required.

It was several days later that Mr Davis was at home and happened to mention how on the day of the big rain the table drain had somehow become blocked and the water had banked up and eventually flooded into their kitchen. 'It was almost as if someone had done it on purpose but nobody around would do a thing like that!' he said, looking at us. 'I would certainly hope not!' Mum said. 'Did it do much damage?' 'Not that much,' he said. 'Peg thought it a good thing. The old linoleum was due to be changed anyway.'

Mrs Davis was another one of those extraordinary women who let it be known: farmer's wives were not to be sat upon.

'That makes three of us now in the valley,' Mum said. 'At least one won't be,' Dad said. 'There would be very few men big enough to successfully sit upon Mrs Davis if she didn't want them to.'

Mrs Davis also drove a car and one day arrived at our place with two friends, one of whom had been sitting in the back seat when Mrs Davis went over a bump. She was jolted high off her seat, her head pressed into the canvas hood and her nose was skinned, from the bridge down, on the roof cross member. She told too how they were crossing a paddock one night in their T Ford when they ran up on a sleeping bull and were stuck there. Mrs Davis was evidently yelling, 'Accelerate the brute!' but they were obliged to suffer the rocking and swaying of the vehicle until the frantic animal, burnt by the hot exhaust, was eventually able to free itself.

The Davises bought a farm, Ross Grange, near Wynyard. We went to see them one Saturday. When we left Mrs Davis was going to get the cows in. 'I won't get much help tonight from Reg,' Mrs Davis said with a laugh. 'He will be listening to the cricket.'

Dad said on the way home that Bill was lucky to have a wife like he had, that he wasn't cut out to be a farmer.

I turned on my carbide lamp and lit a match. And another. Nothing. 'Damn!'

Each Friday, Hong and I rode our bikes the twenty miles from the Burnie High School back home for the weekend. The metal roads were mostly pot-holed or top-dressed with more loose metal.

There was a strong west wind. A head wind. We had been late leaving Burnie.

In June it gets dark early. It was dark by the time we arrived at the Flowerdale turn-off. Hong's generator light

119

was going all right, but mine was a carbide lamp and I had run out of gas.

Going down Medwin's Hill I stuck close behind his back wheel. On the flat next to Charlie Tucker's spuds I came too close, skidded into the loose metal and went flat on my side. Hong stopped and while he was waiting for me to get going again, we heard the raised voices coming from Granny Johnson's house: Hallelujah! Hallelujah!

Granny Johnson had about eight or ten grandchildren going to the Flowerdale School. To me she seemed to be as old as the house she lived in, which was originally the school, moved to its present site well before I was born. It was more like a hall: tall, long and narrow, and the boards were weathered grey. There was a black-boy rose which climbed along a paling fence and onto her porch. It was sometimes covered with masses of dark red flowers.

Mum stopped there once and asked Granny Johnson for a cutting. She was there for a long time and came away with a lot more than she wanted. 'It must be very lonely for her,' Mum had said, 'living there on her own, but she has a lot of relatives who call in often.'

Hong and I had our eyes on the strip of light below the blind. 'Come on!' We put our bikes in the ferns on the side of the road and, like a pair of moths drawn to the light, we sneaked over to sit below the window.

It was some sort of religious meeting with someone talking all the time. We couldn't make a lot of sense out of it all. Jesus, God, Sin and Devil got a lot of mention and someone was interjecting every few minutes to say Amen! or Hallelujah!

Hong decided he would have a peek through the opening below the blind to see if he knew anybody and as he was straightening up to look someone must have pulled a chair back or something, there was a scraping noise on the floorboards and Hong flopped back beside me. Then almost straight away everybody started singing. It was a hymn we had never heard before:

> Lord a little band and lowly;
> We are come to sing to thee;
> Thou art great and high and holy
> O how solemn we should be!

We thought this might be the finish so we hurried back to pick up our bikes before anybody came out. But we could still hear the singing as we rounded the next corner; Hong pedalling pretty fast to keep the generator going so we had some sort of light to see by.

Charlie Brown was the proprietor of the Bottom Pub (more correctly known as the Commercial) in Wynyard. His daughter's name (it always sounded like Icy) was probably Isis. She was regarded as a very good singer and had done well in eisteddfods. She was billed to appear at a concert as the main singer as THE FLORENCE NIGHTINGALE OF THE NORTH WEST COAST!

Cousin Max Hammond often came over from Melbourne to stay on the farm. He brought us the first battery wireless.

He had previously brought with him the bits to make a crystal set, which to us was incredible: to be able to hear a man over two hundred miles across the sea, say: 'This is 3LO Melbourne, the time is . . .' exactly the same as ours. 'Hello, hello, hello – everybody happy? That's the jolly idea . . .'

Then came the battery wireless and two sets of headphones, which meant that four people, although inconvenient, could listen.

And for the cricket!

Neither Mum nor Dad were much concerned about who won the Ashes, whether Bradman or Hammond had made centuries; although I think they were quietly pleased that Hammond kept getting big scores, probably just because Mum's sister had married a Hammond, who could have been a distant relation. And Dad I suppose because he was born in England.

Once when Hong came running out to the kitchen to say that Stan McCabe had just hit Bill Bowes for a six, Mum said, 'Who does Bill Bowes play for?'

Hong was disgusted. 'Aw gee, Mum, you might as well ask who Hornibrook plays for!'

'Hornibrook! What a strange name. Horny – brook. Doesn't really make sense, does it? Is his first name Ivan? You'd wonder some people don't have their names changed by deed poll. Your father had a friend called Agatha Teresa Sidebottom and, would you believe, she lisped; and another called Justin A. Leatherbarrow. I really think some parents, while they may have a moment of fun naming their children forget that the child must carry it with them for –'

'Mum!'

'Oh, sorry. You were saying Mr Hornibrook hit a six.'

'Where's Loch?'

'Boiling up potatoes for the pigs, I think. I saw the copper going.' And seeing Hong disappearing out of the door, 'Did you turn the wireless off, darling?' and turning to me, 'Run and see if he turned it off, will you dear? I don't think Henry heard me.'

'Don't you like cricket, Mum?'

'I don't really know anything about it. It sounds very complicated: long on, second slip, short leg, silly point, maiden over –'

'Mid off –'

'No ball –'

'Gully –'

'Backstop –'

'You don't have backstops in real cricket.'

'You don't! You always tell me to go backstop.'

'That's because we miss a lot behind the wickets. In real cricket the deep fine leg or the third man fields those.'

'Oh, I see. Well run and see if Henry turned the wireless off. You know what Cousin Max said about running the battery down.'

Donald was the third son of F. J. McCabe the rector of the Anglican church in Burnie. Don was my best friend at High School and spent several summer holidays with us at the farm. He loved it: driving the horse in the hay-rake, pitching on to the wagon or on the stack, helping feed pigs, or in the cowshed, hunting rabbits, swimming, or walking through the bush.

Whenever I stayed at the rectory in Burnie we would play tennis or go for a swim if the weather was right but soon Don would start asking about what was happening on the farm, and between us we would organize things for him to come out home.

Don and I were both in F. J's Confirmation classes. Apart from the few things like the Creed which we had to learn off by heart he attempted to give us a little sex education. Because I was very immature and still months away from puberty his warnings about the sins of the flesh left me confused. Often I lay on my back at nights, as he had expressly warned us against, to see what was going to happen, and nothing did. In spite of my friendship with Don, this was a subject I couldn't bring myself to broach with him.

Don was bigger and more clever than I. His hair was dark and uncontrollable, sticking up worse than mine. His sense of humour often had him in trouble with the class teachers.

All my family liked him. I was looking forward to another of his visits.

His older brother, Angus, would be bringing him out after breakfast, early, I would imagine, knowing how they both liked coming, although for quite different reasons, Angus, as much as anything, to talk books with Mum.

On the final morning of Don's last visit I was lying in bed while he stood at the window looking out over the Four Acre to the river. 'Smell the hay,' he said. 'I'll never forget that smell. And I won't forget diving off the bank down at the swimming pool. Or sitting on the gravel with my feet in the water washing the cow muck from between my toes. Or lying on top of a wagon load of hay with nothing up there except the sky.'

I was saying nothing, waiting for him to turn to face me, expecting to see that huge, toothy smile of his. But he was serious. Dead serious. Our eyes met and held and I knew we understood each other. Then I said, 'That reprobate Horsa,' and his face cracked wide open.

Angus, a clever person, who had flown through all his exams, was content to walk about the farm. He had little idea of how to do anything. He was hopeless trying to pitch hay, for instance, whereas Don would pick up any job quickly. Dad said it was common sense, which, he reckoned was the most underrated, and because of that, the most underdeveloped aspect of human intelligence. Sometimes he would go on about it at mealtimes, (and I felt that Mum would keep prodding him just to keep him talking: all work and no play makes Jack a dull boy was one of Mum's favourite sayings) in particular instancing examples of people like professors, economists, highly qualified academics, ('and sadly politicians') who completely lacked common sense. 'Where, for goodness sake, do you find examinations which take into account common sense application of the mind and the body?' I loved hearing him in one of those moods.

Whenever Angus came out, he would go straight in to Mum and if she weren't busy, she would make a cup of tea and they would sit down to talk, about anything; if she were, she would hand Angus a book or a magazine to look at for a minute, and make some comment about some aspect of it. Angus would follow her about the house to continue their discussion.

Once Angus found something which appealed to him. He had just begun to read it out as Don and I walked in. 'Here's an interesting piece from a Miss Dido Carter, London: "The Hengist and Horsa rhyme is incorrectly quoted. The original was written by my brother, the late Desmond Carter, well-known musical comedy and revue lyric writer. As far as I know, it was never published, as it was written for fun in our home.

> Hengist was coarser than Horsa
> and Horsa was awfully coarse
> Horsa drank whiskey,
> told tales that were risque
> but Hengist was in a divorce.
> Horsa grew coarser and coarser
> but Hengist was coarse all his life.
> That reprobate Horsa
> drank tea from a saucer
> but Hengist ate peas with his knife."'

We had all been intrigued to the extent that Don and I had read it over and over and recited it to each other in the paddock.

Probably because I was thinking about Don arriving, the Hengist and Horsa verse came into my head. 'That reprobate Horsa . . .'

When old Jim (he was no carpenter and didn't pretend to

125

be) at last got round to fixing the lavatory seat he proudly
told his wife, who went down to inspect it. She ran her hand
over the boards. 'No splinters. May as well try it out while
I'm here,' she said. She squeezed her huge body through the
door, shut it and sat on the new seat.

Minutes later Jim heard the frantic call for help. Immediately he thought, Snake! and grabbed the snake stick at the
back door and ran. 'Is it still there?' Jim said.

'It grabs me every time I try to stand up.'

'The snake!'

'No idiot, the seat.'

'You mean to say there isn't a snake?'

'Course there's not. This seat, you made. Everytime I go
to stand up it grabs me.

'The seat does? What d'you mean? The seat can't grab
you!'

'You just try it. Ooouch! As soon as I go to stand up it
pinches me.'

'Well look out, I'll come in.'

But Jim couldn't do anything when he got in. There was
barely room to stand beside this big woman with her pants
down around her knees, her dress up and those great thick
thighs reaching almost from one wall to the other. 'Gawd,
you look a one,' Jim said. He couldn't help laughing a bit.

'Never mind that,' she said. 'Do something. Get me out of
here.'

He put one foot up beside her on the back wall and
grabbed her around the waist and pulled.

'That's no good, you fool. I can lift myself. You've got
t' stop the boards pinching when I take the weight off. Get
an axe or something and cut the boards.'

'Cut the boards! Gawd, woman, it took us half a day to
put 'em there. I'm not cutting 'em orf. Not yet, I'm not. I got
an idea though. Just sit there for a bit, while I go around the
back.'

'Round the back? You can't do nothin' round the back.'
But Jim had gone.

He opened the trap door and carefully pulled out the pan.
He got down on his hands and knees, twisted his head inside
the hole and looked up.

'Jesus!'

'What's up?'

'What's up! You oughta see yourself!'

'There's nothin' to laugh about. Get on with it or I'll pee
on you.'

'You do an' I'll bloody leave you there. Gawd, you look a
sight! Look Bet, when I say GO you lift up an' I'll see where
you're caught. Right? GO!'

'Ooooch!'

'Did you lift? I didn't see nothin' move. An' I can't feel
nothin'. Wait 'till I get me matches.'

'What are you doin', down there. Go an' get an axe or
something.'

'Don't get excited. We'll have you out in two ups.' Jim
pulled the matches out of his pocket, held the box up and lit
a match.

Everything happened simultaneously. Bet screamed. There
was a noise inside like a wild poddycalf was let loose in the
shed. There was the sound of a board lifting and slapping
back into position. There was (down where Jim was) the
acrid smell of burnt hair. And above him a hole through
which he stupidly poked his head.

Surprisingly, it only took a few days before Bet and Jim
were able to entertain anyone who wanted to hear the full
story. They thoroughly enjoyed the notoriety it afforded.

'. . . more fool me,' Jim might say, 'I stuck me head up the
hole to see what was goin' on and Wham she got me. With
all the cussing and me ears ringing I backed outa that hole
quicker than a lobster an' took off . . .'

And Bet would break in with that big laugh of hers.

'Backed out's right! He bowled the pan clean over – all that mess. I left everything fair where it was until he eventually come 'ome and I made 'im bury it right there and plant a rhubarb on the spot as a memory . . .'

And if you asked about the boards, did they fix them? They would laugh and Bet would tell you how she tacked a rabbit skin over the crack. 'I reckon it'd have t'be the most comfortable dunny seat in Flowerdale, now.'

THE SKYLARK

On the first day of the Christmas holidays, after one year at High School, Bern awoke to a feeling of melancholia, almost claustrophobic, with the dark walls and ceilings pressing in on him. He looked through the bottom half of the window below the yellow blind. The bit of sky he could see beside the huge, spreading pine tree, was clear and bright enough, but it gave no comfort. In fact he was content to stare at the drabness of his room, to swim for a bit in a pool of dejection.

'The boy's exhausted,' Bern heard his mother say, when his father came in for breakfast. 'I'll let him sleep.'

Loch had come in to see if he wanted to help them burn rushes down in the creek, but he had no wish to go and feigned a headache. He waited until he heard them all leave the house before he got up and dressed.

After a light breakfast he wandered off aimlessly, listlessly, across the grass paddocks.

He found himself sitting in a patch of long grass and clover in a cow paddock. His mind was so filled with thoughts, or emptied of them, that he was not conscious of how he had come to be there.

He watched the plumes of smoke rising from the pyramidal heaps of grubbed rushes, and his brothers carrying torches of fire from one heap to another.

He lay in the grass staring up at the clouds, which had always fascinated him with their shapes and movements; the exquisite ethereal quality of a power as vague and mysterious as religion.

It had been a big year, a moving out into a new stream, swifter, deeper, and more unpredictable than the slow, familiar currents of his earlier years. Rather like the clouds, he mused, changing in shape and pattern; and moving, always moving, disappearing beyond the horizon; only ever returning in a different form.

Yes! like the clouds. Sometimes drifting, other times with the wind behind them tearing them to bits.

That first day! Riding his bike into Wynyard to catch the rail motor. Mr Hicks, the driver, waiting for a minute at the end of Jackson Street, while he, and another boy he had never seen before, ran to clamber on board. Big Lyell Ewington, the perfect: 'Move over, Cameron!' 'I've got a handle to my name!' 'I know. Most mugs have handles. Move over, Mug!'

The chatter. The giggles. Shouts of welcome as they stopped at various places to pick up another lot.

Then the rail motor disgorging its load of green uniformed children at the school stop. He had followed the moving stream into the grounds. Unknown and alone he had found his way to the lavatory. He watched two boys capture blowflies on a frosted window, festooned with spiders' webs. Outside he watched them threading grass stems through the bodies of the flies, throwing them into the air, to watch them, wings flailing, struggle to remain airborne; recapturing the unsuccessful ones and trimming back the length of straw.

Bern had watched as one, accompanied by the laughter of its tormentors, nosedived and crashed at his feet. Deliberately, he raised his boot and crushed it.

They had backed him against the wall. 'What'd you do that for?' The bigger boy tapped Bern's forehead with the butt of his palm, so his head cracked against the brickwork.

'What'd you do it for?' the other boy said. 'It was ours. It wasn't yours.'

'He doesn't answer,' the bigger boy said, and thumped his head again. Much as Bern had tried to control his feelings, the pain brought tears to his eyes.

Then Alf Burrows had ridden around the corner on his bike. 'Leave the kid alone,' he said, seeing immediately what was happening. The two boys turned, grinned sheepishly and walked off; then, as if a sudden thought had impelled them, they ran, shouting to someone across the playground.

Bern watched them go. The boy with the bike said, 'Do you know them?' Bern shook his head.

'They're all right, just first day back at school, you know. What's your name?'

'Bern.' (He would hide Scrub as long as he could.)

'I'm Alf. Have you got any friends here?'

'No.'

'Where do you come from? What school?'

'Flowerdale.'

'Flowerdale. Oh, I know. I went fishing there once with my dad. Do you ever go fishing?'

'Often.'

'You're lucky. Have you got a proper rod?'

'We make them out of dogwood, but mostly we lie on the willow branches and hold the line in our fingers. If you lie quiet enough and get the light right you can see the fish like in a tank. Blackfish, that is.'

Alf put his bike in the bike shed and slipped off his trouser clips. He stood up. He was smiling. 'As I said, you're real lucky to be able to go fishing like you do. Any more kids from Flowerdale here?'

'No.'

'Then come with me, Bern. I'll show you around a bit.'

They walked together across the quadrangle, Alf, recognized and greeted on all sides, the new boy, at least noticed.

The school was so different from Flowerdale, where children stayed, according to law, until the day they turned fourteen; where one teacher taught five different classes in one room; where learning was a tiresome drudgery imposed on children by grownups, to keep them out of the way until they were old enough to work. At High School there were different classrooms for different subjects, and many teachers, all of whom wore long, black gowns. And children! He had never seen so many children together at a time, except when he had gone to Melbourne to stay with his aunt at Pascoe Vale and had seen the local school playground at lunchtime swarming with children, like ants, hundreds of them, and running here and there as aimlessly, without any apparent purpose.

There were compensations. He had made several good friends including Don McCabe, the incorrigible and lovable son of the Burnie C of E parson, and Col Daking who lived on a farm at Table Cape.

Don lent him a racquet and taught him to play tennis. And for the second time he would be coming out to stay on the farm after Christmas.

The weekend English homework of an essay, which most of the other students hated, Bern looked forward to. Not that he often received very high marks: five, six, or seven was the usual, but once an 'Excellent – 9/10' thrilled him.

And when Mr Fletcher, the inspector (he had a habit of spraying the front rows with spittle as he talked) was taking their class for English, and asked if anyone disagreed with an answer to a question on the parsing of a sentence, Bern had, with considerable trepidation, raised his hand, and with the cold blue eyes of the inspector on him, as well as those of his class mates, he had apologetically given his opinion, to be told that he was the only one right. And later during the same lesson it had happened again; and when, to his embarrassment, he found he was again the only dissenter, Mr Fletcher had said, 'Come on Professor, tell them.'

But this had had its natural reaction. His mediocrity in other subjects, particularly mathematics and science, often found him with the wrong answer and several times he had become aware of the whispered comment and the sniggering that followed, 'Come on, Professor, tell 'em,' so that he wished he had never had his moment of triumph.

Because of occasional asthma attacks, he had been forced to withdraw from many sporting activities, and the fact that he was one of the smallest and probably the least developed, sexually, in his class, his sense of inferiority was magnified.

It made it difficult for him to talk freely with the girls, as other boys did, without blushing or stammering, and always, it seemed, to be followed by an unreasonable anger at his own inadequacies.

He adored Eve Cowdrey, a girl from another class, from a distance. He had dropped one of his books in the corridor and she had picked it up and handed it to him. And smiled. In his confusion he could find no adequate words to thank her.

He had watched for her at recess and dinnertimes and cursed himself on those occasions when she suddenly appeared, and he must turn away from her. He had wondered then if she had ever noticed the colour creeping up his neck and cheeks. Or noticed him at all.

The first time he remembered seeing her and always afterwards, her face had reminded him of the face of a girl he had seen before somewhere: the swept-back, golden hair, the wide forehead, the large, brown eyes. Or perhaps it was a painting by one of the great artists.

The feeling persisted, and one afternoon in the library, when he was idly thumbing through an art book, he had come across the painting: 'Head of a Child' by Rubens. The likeness was remarkable. He lay the book on the floor, and on his knees, with his chin cupped in his hands, he studied it.

The child was younger of course, but there was a marked similarity apart from the colour of her hair and her eyes. The chin and the cheeks were too wide and too coloured. Eve's face was white, almost milk white, and the nose and the chin were more pointed, but the soft, round eyes and full lips were similar, and, he thought, both were very beautiful.

Bern had been unaware of her presence, until he heard her voice. 'Hullo,' she said, 'what are you studying?'

The sudden surge of happiness which had swept over him was followed immediately by the panic of a cornered rabbit. He glanced quickly at her, and away, immersed in his guilt. 'Art,' was all he could say.

She had knelt on one knee beside him and stared at the picture. 'Hmmm, Rubens. Ve-ery nice. And look, she's got fair hair and brown eyes. Don't you think she's a bit like me?'

He felt the slight pressure of her shoulder against his. He saw the white flesh of her thigh. Her nearness thrilled him.

'Do you like art, Bern?' So easy and natural! And she knew his name.

He wondered if she heard his whispered 'Yes'. And tried to ask: 'Do you?' but no words came.

She stood up then and said as she walked along the shelves: 'Miss Kiddle said I should read any of John Buchan's.' She held up a book. 'Do you know this one, *Huntingtower*?'

'I've only read *Greenmantle*,' Bern heard himself saying. And was amazed at the steadiness of his voice.

'I'll take *Huntingtower*,' she said, 'and let you know what I think of it.' She smiled then and left him.

Two weeks later she had told him. He was going to join some boys at lunch time when she called him. She was lying with a girl friend on the grass, on her stomach, her elbows and knees on the ground, her feet in the air. 'Hey, Bern,' she called. He was drawn to her and must kneel on the grass a little away from the two girls. 'I finished that book,' she said.

'It's about some Scottish boys from the slums – the Gorbals Diehards. You'd enjoy it.' Then speaking through a large bite of sandwich, 'Have you heard, I'll be leaving at the end of term. Dad has been transferred to a bank in Hobart.'

'You're leaving!' Bern said. He could not believe what she was saying. She was leaving! Since their chance meeting in the library, he had thought about her constantly. And he had hoped – Yet she could say it so brightly. So casually. As if she wanted to go. 'I must read it,' Bern said.

She laughed. 'Oh, you mean the book! But aren't you sorry I'm going?'

He stood up, knowing the blood was rushing to his face, and this time, inexplicably, not caring, not turning away, 'Of course I'm sorry,' he said angrily. And could say no more to the girl who would torture him; and in front of her friend. For a moment he stared at the shoes which clicked idly above her bottom, then at the golden swept-back hair, and at the laughing brown eyes, which would haunt him. 'I'd better go and have my lunch,' Bern said. 'The boys'll be wondering. Good luck, Eve.'

It was the first time he had addressed her by her name. As he moved away he heard Eve Cowdrey say something, and the two girls burst out laughing. He knew, damn it, that they were laughing at him, or about him.

Bern felt the sun beating down on his face. He watched a long, white cloud, a greyhound running, gradually shifting across the blue of the sky, losing its form in skeins of white lace. The breeze touched his hair and eyebrows, blowing the scent of clover to his nostrils, nodding the heads of cocksfoot grass. A bee droned a few inches from his head. He shut his eyes and drifted with the cloud. With the stretching, straining hound.

The skylark hadn't wakened him. Unless it was the bird's

wing which had brushed his cheek, and not the wind. It was just above him when its song began. Its wings flapped, treading air. It moved upwards in a wide circle, its song never faltering. The notes poured out, tumbling over each other, saturating the air, dripping, dropping around him.

Bern watched the bird move up. Around and up. Singing. Upwards. Up and up. Its flapping wings, mechanical bellows, pressed out an endless stream of notes.

The bird was becoming smaller. A spot. A speck. A tiny black dot. A nothing. And still the confetti of sound continued. He squeezed shut his eyes. Listening. The sky, the black sky, shattered into a thousand jewels, five pointed jewels of sound.

He opened his eyes. Wide. Searching for the bird. The bird that was not there. That was. Because the song was there.

The greyhound panting on a bed of straw.

Then he saw it. A moving speck on the dog's white tail. He wondered if it was still climbing. How long could the heart and the throat of the bird continue?

Such perfect song!

He watched it continue to move in a circle. Slowly in a circle. What caused it to sing? To fly so high? To sing so beautifully? And for so long? And for whom? Who listened?

He raised himself on his elbows and searched the paddock around him. Cattle were there. Were they listening? Would they notice if it stopped? Or if it started again?

Was this bird's song (like the ticking of the diningroom clock) just a part of all that he loved – of what was real and solid – like the piece of tin his mum and dad kept taking out and putting in the stove – like Bassett's hill – or the river – or the nightly readings (he missed those while at school) – everything about security?

The nearest cow was lying with one foreleg stretched out, its head high, its ears erect, eyes closed, its mouth chewing rhythmically, the cud it chewed swallowed down into the gut (you could see the ripple on the neck hair) to make way for a new one. Perhaps she was listening?

Perhaps the lark sang only for him? (And, of course, for other people who listened.) Had it been proved that the lark ever sang when nobody was there to listen?

If only she could hear it. If only everyone could hear it; to be forced to lie here on their backs, here, like he was now, with the clover smell, and the cow noises, and the clouds, and the skylark singing. How could it then be possible to go away and be cruel to each other?

The lark was bigger now. It was coming down. Down. Down. A short distance above him its song ceased. He wanted to hold out his hands to catch the last notes. It folded its wings close against its body and dropped like a dead thing, until, just above him, (he felt he could have touched it) it spread its wings and drifted over onto a post.

It stood there with ruffled feathers, looking at him. He wanted to speak, to say: well done! He wanted to clap. But couldn't. He must not move. He breathed short shallow breaths through a slit of mouth, conscious not to allow his chest to move.

The bird was content. There was nothing to worry about. It lifted a wing and preened its feathers with a sharp beak. Suddenly it was an ordinary bird. Brown. Sandy-brown. Small. Ordinary. Except for that very long hind claw. And, of course, its song.

It moved closer. A jump along the wire fence. Another jump. Almost above him now. A very ordinary bird. Except for its eye. It fluttered down. It was within his reach. But out of his vision. Slowly he raised his head.

The bird sensed his first movement. It flew off on one wing, (shamming the other broken) lop-sided, coaxing him to follow.

He swung over on to his knees and saw the nest cunningly

placed in a clump of grass. Almost hidden.

He wondered that the cows, or he, had not trodden on it.

Two heads lifted, two beaks opened wide as his fingers brushed the grass. He stared down into their throats. He took his hand away and waited until the baby larks had settled down again.

The bird had flown back on the fence, not far from him. The cow had stopped chewing. She was watching him. She flicked one ear. Her eye-lashes were long and curled and ginger.

Another lark across the paddock had started to sing. He could see the bird's wings fluttering. The one that was on the fence had gone. The cow was still watching him, indifferently, monitoring his movements.

He looked down to the creek. The plumes of smoke were lifting, almost vertically, and joining in a loose cloud that floated towards the south. His brothers were still busy lighting fires. He saw Loch with a brand of burning rushes, held out from his body, away from the wind, his left arm held up to protect his face from the jumping flames, running full pelt to thrust the flames into the bottom of a new mound of rushes.

Everything was perfect: the warm sun, the clouds, the cows, his brothers with their fires, the smoke, the larks singing.

Almost he was fooled. His wishful thinking that she could see, and hear, and take notice!

Probably she would not care about larks. Only one person in a thousand would ever stop to hear a lark. Even most of the country people who heard wouldn't listen. It would mean nothing.

All this – this beauty. It was unreal. Unnatural. False. There was cruelty. Everywhere. People were cruel. He knew that now. In the real world people were cruel.

Here in the country he was sheltered from life as it really

was. Cows, larks – the sky, the clouds, the winds – to sing until they had no more breath for singing, to make nests, to lay eggs, to hatch their young. But *people*!

He looked down at the fledgelings in their nest, warm and waiting to be fed, trusting. He brushed his fingers over them. Two part-feathered heads with paper-thin skins and big eyes lifted. Two bills opened wide expectantly. An anger built up in him. Suddenly! That amidst all this he could be so miserable! An anger that swelled and overflowed like milk boiling.

She was the cause of it all. She, the girl he had worshipped, had, last night at the end of year social, ignored him. Twice he had tried to approach her, but she had remained the radiant centre of a group that would not admit him.

He raised his hand and brought it down, a clenched fist, on the two birds. Again. And again.

For a few seconds he stared at the blood and slime on his hand and then at the carnage that a few moments before was two birds in a nest. His breathing was the deep chest-heaving of the asthmatic, but subsiding with the realization of what he had done.

He wiped his hand carefully on the grass. He took his knife and dug a hole in the turf and buried the birds. He covered the place where the nest had been with a cowpat. He looked at the fist that had crushed the birds, spat on it and scrubbed it into the dirt, and wiped it at last on the grass, removing any vestige of evidence of the act.

He stood up. On the other side of the paddock he saw a lark still lifting into a spiral climb. Its song carried to him loud and clear on a warm wind. For some time he stood watching it. Listening. Then slowly he walked down past the resting cows towards the creek where his brothers were burning rushes.

Already he could smell the familiar, acrid smell of the smoke from rush fires. Pleasant. Satisfying. Behind, faintly

139

now, he could hear a lark singing. He cupped his hands and shouted. Loch and Henry heard and waved. He waved back and suddenly he was running down to them.

CHRISTMAS AT CURRAJONG

It must have been because the weather was fine and Dad had three paddocks of hay already cut and carted into a stack in the Four Acre, and because tomorrow was Christmas Day, that Dad was happy to let Hong and me take Kit in the sledge up to the Blackwood Creek to get manfern fronds.

Loch caught and harnessed Kit for us. Kit was a half draught and had boundless energy. Too much, normally, it seemed, for us to be trusted to take him on our own. 'He's a bit flighty,' Dad would say. 'Perhaps you'd better take Bonney.' But this time he said, 'Yes, all right, but drive carefully and don't leave him anywhere without tying him up. I'll get Loch to catch and harness him for you.'

Bob often told the story of how he and Kit had moulded seven acres of potatoes in a day and at the end of it Kit had cantered with Bob on his back all the way to the stable. 'There's not another horse 'ud lay a candle to Kit when it comes to moulding or scarifying spuds.' Bob would smile knowingly, and shake his head.

Loch handed the reins to us with a warning, 'Don't forget, it's Kit you've got and not Bonney.'

We took off quietly enough with me holding back on the reins. Judy came running out of the garden gate and jumped on the back of the sledge with Hong. I held Kit in until we got to the top of the house paddock then I said, 'Hang on,' and flipped the reins. Hong and Jude grabbed each other and went rolling off the back of the sledge.

I did a circle and they clambered on again, grinning like idiots. 'Why didn't you warn us?'

But I had. 'Hang on, I said. Didn't you hear me?'

'Yeah, after we fell off.'

'Then hang on, this time!' And away we went again in another wide circle, with Hong and Judy on the floor and holding on to me, so if one went the lot would. We were all laughing and Kit seemed to be enjoying himself. For all our speeding it took us longer to get to the creek than it would have done if we had taken plodding old Bonney, although she would trot too if urged enough. Canter even. But so clumsily, and when you stopped her eventually, she would accuse you with her eyes, and you'd feel ashamed and sorry and want to hug her great thick hairy neck.

We tied Kit up to a blackwood growing close by the creek and set off to get manfern fronds. Hours, days, weeks of our lives had been spent down there in the creek bed. Apart from the odd blackwood tree the dark, furry trunks of the manferns were the only support for the wide and low green roof which let in only stray patches of sunshine.

With the creek chuckling low-key around roots and stones, black, shiny-black, been there for ever, it was easy for us to believe in magic; easy to forget there was a real world out there somewhere.

It was especially good to have Judy back with us too. Since she had won a bursary two years before to attend the Methodist Ladies College in Launceston, we only saw her on holidays. We showed her a hut which we had built from broken limbs, lined and walled with manfern fronds threaded through branches. Because they were all dead and powdery we spent an hour pulling the old ones out and replacing them with fresh green ones.

We loaded the sledge and sitting on the pile of ferns set off·

for the house. 'Gee, it's good to be home,' Jude said. 'I like it all right at school – some of the girls – but it's good to come back. There're a couple of teachers – oooh, anyway – forget them. It's good to be home.' She laughed.

I knew what she meant. I had just completed my first year at High School; only four days in the week boarding, and not in a city like Launceston, and ours was a mixed school, mixed sexes that is, while hers was all girls.

She was a bit of a tomboy. But I suppose with four brothers and no sisters, she had to be. She could do most things we did. She was a good shot with a rifle and not bad with a shanghai. And climb trees. I couldn't imagine what it would be like at her school in Launceston boarding with all those girls.

Jude and I were sitting on the load with our feet hanging down over the back. It was all right for Jude because she was wearing shoes and socks, but when Hong ran over a thistle I copped it in both feet. He laughed, which made me think he had done it on purpose.

With my chin between my knees, I began pulling out thorns. He flipped the reins and yelled out, 'Hang on!' as I grabbed Jude and the two of us went flying. I rolled over. I couldn't stop myself from laughing. Until I suddenly caught sight of Jude lying there on her back. It was only for a second or two. My hand must have caught her blouse as I grabbed her, either undoing or ripping off a button, for there it was winking at me, one of her breasts, the brown surround of the nipple and the small but definite swelling in the raw.

My own sister! Of course she was two years older than me, but somehow she was still the same tomboy sister, but now – she would never be the same.

What was happening to me? Why should the sight of this part of a girl's body suddenly startle me? I suppose because it was so secret, so mysterious. To talk about it was taboo, except with the boys at school, my only source of sexual knowledge, which added to the mystery and confusion.

It was strange too that I was becoming much more aware, of people. Situations seemed to arise by accident. Like clutching at Judy like that, the two of us falling, she on her back with her breast bare and within a few inches of me. Like recently when Daphne Goodwin was staying with us and we were down swimming and messing about in a tin canoe Hong and I had made, and Daphne had asked me to let her have a ride.

Because the canoe could be easily tipped over I had asked her to sit very still with her legs apart, one up each side and facing me. Her swimming togs were slack and as I pushed off from the bank I looked down at her crotch to see her micky, plainly visible, with golden hairs shining in the sunlight.

There would be no possible escape from it for the duration of our tour up the river and back and even more embarrassing, what was going to happen to me if something wasn't done, and done very quickly? I leaned a little too far to one side and over we went – me to cool off in the never-too-warm Flowerdale water, Daphne, no doubt wondering if she really had caused the thing to capsize.

I tore my eyes away from Jude's breast, but she had noticed, she would have to have noticed my sudden change of humour. I sat there beside her concentrating on a prickle in my foot while Hong came flying back in a wide circle to pick us up. I looked up. He was laughing uncontrollably.

'Didn't you hear me say, "Hang on"?'

I couldn't help laughing too. But Jude, I noticed, wasn't amused now. I looked at her chin which she had so often ground into my spine, and at her blouse. The button had not been ripped off at all. 'Right,' she said, 'it's my turn to drive.' It was. And I was pleased. Hong knew it was too and made no protest. He sat on the back with me. 'Did you get a prickle in your foot?' With that smirking grin.

Before I could answer, without warning, Jude had Kit in a

canter. Hong grabbed at me but I was ready this time and pushed him over the back. It made me feel a lot better to see him roll over and over. Divots, cut out by the horse's feet were flying past as we did two long circles before we pulled up to pick up our lost passenger.

'Did you fall off?' Jude had regained her sense of humour.

We drove up to the garden gate and I held Kit while Jude and Hong unloaded. Kit kept pushing his nose into my chest.

'I'll come and help you unharness,' Jude said. She was taller than me and could reach the hames and collar straps without standing on a box. As I undid the winkers, Kit pulled her head back, turned and galloped up the paddock.

We walked back to the house together and Jude asked me about High School. I knew then that whatever she or I thought about what had happened, neither or us would be saying anything. I felt grateful and a little smug that I could share a confidence with her, secret, as it would remain.

It took a long time to drape the verandah walls and hang the few festive decorations in the dining room and passage.

And this year was another landmark. There would be no Christmas stockings, (a sock packed with a few relatively useless items and dates and raisins and nuts to keep everybody quiet for a while). Apart from that the day would begin much as I had always remembered it: early milking; dress in clean clothes, face and hands scrubbed, hair wet and combed, ready for breakfast; ready for the presents. Never did we have a Christmas tree. The gifts were prepared sometimes days before and carefully wrapped and stacked away in our cupboards: a pound of nails for Dad, a jam dish for Mum, things unimaginative or expendable but which always won the enthusiastic approval of the recipient. 'Exactly what I wanted!'

145

The places at the table piled high with gifts, always more interesting in their wrappings – breakfast half-eaten, 'Mum, look, he put his paper in my porridge!' with a giggle; bacon curled up and cold, 'Hey, I want that.'; toasting fork sitting on the spike on the stove door with a half-inch thick slice of black carbon on the prongs. 'This yours, Jude?' an inch away from her nose.

But happy! Everybody happy. Particularly when the scrawled note is at last unearthed inside a series of fake wrappings: 'For Scrub and Hong, look under a horse rug, under one of the feed troughs in the stable. Love from Frank.' But the voice of reason: 'Wait a moment! Have you finished your breakfast?' And the billy-cart must wait a little longer.

Yes, Frank is back! There's an aura of mystery about him too. He had passed his 'banker's exam' at Perry's, where he and Loch had attended private tuition. But after the bank crash, after the Buchans and all the others working in the branches that closed throughout Tasmania, there was no job for him. When he turned eighteen he left Loch to help Dad on the farm and went off on his own to explore the great unknown.

With little more than enough money to pay his fare on the *Oonah* to get him to Melbourne, he left home and joined the body of unemployed. His occasional letters read as exciting episodes of a serial. Particularly that first year, when everything to us was so extraordinary, so different.

Sometimes we waited for hours, from the time the letter arrived until, as Mum suggested, everybody was seated around the tea table at night, when the seal was broken and the news read out loud.

Dad's and Mum's reactions to some of the bald accounts of Frank's adventures were, at first, puzzling. Dad, often silent, except perhaps for a deep sigh, would shake his head and stare into the fire; while Mum, quite often would laugh spontaneously and perhaps add, 'But, Kay, he's young. It (whatever it was) won't hurt him!'

I would look from one to the other, completely bemused, trying to take in the implications of 'hiding under a tarpaulin on a good's train' '. . . Mr Hugh Murray, a dour old bloke with an acre of bananas, on an eighteen acre farm with a boarding house in Gympie. The bathroom is floored with dirty, greasy planks. He's got a half-bred dingo dog which he will back to beat any Alsatian . . .' 'Mrs Cheshire is very kind, five feet by five feet, as tall as she is round . . .'

Then he had walked into the Cedar Hotel at Finch Hatton. 'Mr Keating, a gentleman publican, moved in only three days before I arrived and gave me a job for a week as yardman . . . They are like a second family and have given me a room in the attic for weekends. In exchange I cut wood, look after the kero engine which is used for lighting and help run the picture theatre on Saturdays. During the week I work (very hard) cutting cane – live in a kanaka hut on the job during the week. A big carpet snake lives in the roof – funny to look up when you're in bed to see him/her staring down at you. One eighteen footer lives under a shed – see them in the cane, usually smallish – take them by the tail and throw them out of the way. Good ratters so we don't kill them.'

So the saga continued: exciting, interesting, worrying, light-hearted. 'Contracted double pneumonia in Melbourne, spent six delirious days in the Salvo Bethesda Hospital –' 'Vince Middleton and I bought a 1929 Dodge Sedan from Mr Keating for one hundred pounds. Got our own labels printed and sold a few bottles of ink, did some fencing and odd jobs in the back country down as far as Dalby. Made no money, but paid for petrol and expenses. Vince coming down for a holiday after Christmas, if that's all right. You'll like Vince. Perhaps he could get a job somewhere for a week or two at Amberley or Hardy Wilson might want some fencing done?'

147

Yes, Frank was back. At least for a while, before he would come in someday to say casually to Mum, 'I think I'll go back to the other side on Saturday.' Which meant he had already booked his passage. And Mum would fuss to see that all his clothes were in order. Which was no big problem because she had been expecting him to go off again soon anyway.

And Mum would tell Dad. And Dad would say, 'Hmmmm.'

Frank was back; with his ideas on political reform, his Social (Douglas) Credit ideas.

Always, when we were waiting for his arrival, I would be reminded of the parable, which Mum had often read us, about the prodigal son. All the excitement! Even Dad kept saying things like: 'When Frank is here' or 'I must show Frank –'

But it wasn't the same because we never killed a fatted calf and anyway although he had gone off to a far country he hadn't 'wasted his substance with riotous living'. But I did wonder a bit whether Loch ever thought about it at all, because he was always there, helping Dad on the farm and doing things for Mum, and keeping a beautiful vegie garden. But I don't think he did think about it because he was always as excited as anyone to have his older brother back again.

Mum came up to see what we had done with the manferns and raved a bit about how good it looked, which made us feel pleased.

I could see Frank with the push mower going around and around the lawn by the verandah. I knew he must have mown the big lawn out the front. He could do in an hour what it always took Hong and me at least a day and about six drinks of raspberry vinegar to finish.

Loch, Mum told us, was getting the cricket pitch ready for tomorrow's game. And Dad was scything all the long grass there. 'I must get him to clean up around the magnolia tree,'

Mum said, 'and along the laurels, and all those rough edges – oh, and Jude dear, I must ask you to give me a hand in the kitchen – you've all done a wonderful job here – and boys, perhaps you'd get a rake and a bag or wheelbarrow and cart off the grass your father has mown, and is going to mow – I hope – if he is not distracted – this time of year – oh, and would you bring in some more wood, blackwood small wood; I'm afraid I'm using quite a lot with all this cooking.'

As we moved out Mum said to Judy. 'You've done that beautifully, darling. You know we may be poor but we do practise a shabby gentility.'

Hong said that he would get the wood if I went off to rake the grass. I stopped at the garden gate and stared down at our cricket pitch. It was looking good already. Loch had both sets of wickets in, wickets which he had made from straight dogwood and skinned the bark off so they were shiny white. I knew we had the good willow bat Dad had made and then as a spare we had the not-so-good one Hong and I had made; and according to previous practice, one of us should get a new cricket ball from Mum and Dad for Christmas.

Loch was starting to paint in the crease lines with white-wash. Dad was scything in an ever-widening rectangle from the pitch. Whenever I tried to use the scythe I seemed to either mow too low or too high or stick the point into the ground, but Dad had that easy rhythm and sweep which left a smooth almost perfect finish with the cut grass lined up in a neat row on the left side.

'Years of practice,' he said once. 'I always got the job at home at Woodrising of mowing the tennis court for the family.'

I ran down the hill with the rake, Hong would come belting down soon with the barrow. I would need to have Dad's rows all heaped up ready.

I was hoping as usual for a fine Christmas. The Johnstons as always would be out for the day. I knew exactly what would happen. They would arrive before dinner. Evy, my cousin, (much older than me – she had gone overseas with the soldiers in the Great War as a Sister) would go straight inside to help Mum and Jude with the final preparations for the big meal.

George, a returned soldier, their two sons, Bob and Peter, and baby Helen, (who only recently had been hidden inside Evy's large round tummy – something which had filled me with awe, sitting next to her at the table) were left to wait to be called for any help needed.

The dinner, a party affair, was food and more food, paper hats from inside bonbons, and gifts carefully wrapped in coloured paper, (which was folded and afterwards stacked away for future use); the pudding with threepences and the odd sixpence; the reading out of jokes; the glass of wine for the grownups, which both Mum and Dad seemed to make last the whole meal; the cigarette which Dad was given and which he held like he would a pencil, never seeming to be able to escape the sting of smoke curling up into his eyes.

And constant attention for one of George's droll remarks; like when Dad mentioned three brothers called Nelson, Horatio and Victor. 'If there had been any more sons,' George said, 'I suppose they would have started on England expects . . .'

I tried repeating some of George's jokes because they tickled me, but I rarely found anyone who thought them funny. Yet we had all laughed when George told them. Perhaps it was George. Perhaps it was just Christmas. Is that what Christmas is all about? 'On earth, peace, good will toward men.' 'Men!' said Mum, crossing out the last word on a Christmas message and replacing it with 'all'. 'One can understand Luke, but one would think Mr Longfellow would have had more sense!'

TAKE IT AS SHE COMES

By the third year of High School he had sorted himself out. He had managed to make the firsts in football and skinned his knees on the gravel at the Queenstown oval. He had scraped into the first tennis squad for one inter-high match and once was twelfth man for the cricket firsts. He finished the school year by getting nine passes out of nine, no credits, no distinctions.

In the three years his horizons had exploded; not just his schooling. He had met and made friends with boys and girls from town and country with varied backgrounds, and that first year he had boarded with working men: Charlie, Len, and Aub. They talked about a wider world than the one he had known.

He liked them all, but especially Aub. He liked his happy, friendly manner, his fresh and genuine philosophy: 'My old man used to say: "If you've got a stone in your boot, don't curse the stone, thank your stars you've got a boot for it t' get in".' 'Check the weather out and dress according,' I say. 'No point wearing an oilskin when it's hot and sunny. Now is there, Robbie? Take it as she comes,' I say.

'The best game I ever played,' he said one day, not just to Bern (and he had played some good ones for the Burnie Tigers) 'was when I had a root in the loft above the dressing room just before the game.'

The nonchalant matter-of-factness of the statement startled the boy; and that it had been said at the table. (Admittedly only men, and a boy, present.) To hide his confusion, Bern was concentrating on loading some peas onto his fork when Aub continued, 'If you're hungry and you can get the tucker, eat it; if you're thirsty and there's drink about, drink. Wouldn't you reckon, Robbie?'

(He liked the way Aub had called him Robbie from the beginning. 'What's your name?' 'Bern.' 'Do you like it?' 'Not particularly.' 'Have you got a nickname?' He didn't mind Scrub at home, but not here; a few of the kids at school now called him Robbie. 'Robbie.' 'Then Robbie it is.')

But as Mrs Davis walked in with a tray of sweets, Aub turned to her. 'What do you think Mrs D?'

'About what?'

'If you're hungry, eat. If you're thirsty, drink.'

'That's if you're lucky enough to get it. There's plenty can't.'

'That's right,' Aub said. 'That's exactly what I was saying, wasn't it Robbie? If you're lucky enough to get it, go for it.'

The others were looking at Bern, smiling at his embarrassment. But Mrs Davis had gone again. She had more to do than bandy words with her boarders.

One day, after school, Bern got his bike out to go for a ride. The day was sunny but a strong wind blew from the south. He had had a bad day at school, both Malone and Belbin, the maths and science masters, had been cranky, not just with him, with the whole class.

He stood on the footpath, with the bike leaning against his hip while he fixed his trouser clips. Mr Cherry, from a few houses along, was talking with Inspector Jones who looked out of character with a pair of secateurs in one hand and a bunch of roses in the other. He felt them watching him as he skidded across the road and sped off down the hill past Pegus's shop.

The frustrations of the day left him. He felt the wind gusts at the cross streets, trying to force him off the road. Waves kept hurling into the breakwater. Against the wind he could hear only a dull roar of the sea but as each wave broke he could see the water spray, a white wall, reaching high in the air and falling back on itself.

Down past the railway station, along Marine Terrace, the wind head-on. He didn't lean forwards and down to dodge it, but stood on his pedals, taking it, feeling the force of it making his eyes water. His breath came deep and heavy, lifting his shoulders, but it wasn't a wheeze so much as the result of asthma. He felt an exhilaration from the effort. He would go as far as the old Round Hill Butter Factory and return.

Turning east, the wind was hitting him side-on, gusting, as if it would catch him unawares and throw him, bike and all, down over the sand dunes into the chop and sparkle of water hissing, in spite of the wind, far up the yellow sand.

From a long way back he saw the linesmen. He passed one, leaning over the tray of the truck. He appeared to be screwing insulators on to a cross-bar. The second man was at the top of a telegraph pole. The wind was plucking at his shirt and trousers, and his hair was streaming seawards. There was something familiar about the figure, supported, at a forty-five degree angle, by a belt around the waist to the centre of the cross-bar, and boot-spikes driven into the wooden pole, while he tied wires to insulator cups.

As he came nearer, he recognized the man as Aub Johnston: Aub, the footballer, who could fly high above the packs for his marks, Aub, the joker, who never consciously hurt anybody, Aub, whose fundamental wisdom could not be learned in schools.

The boy stopped, resting on his bike, with one foot over the bar on a pedal, the other on the metal road. One arm, he held like a broken wing, thumb resting on his forehead, shielding the sun from his eyes.

Unbidden the picture on Mrs Davis's wall, above the foot of the table, where Aub always sat, came into his mind. A stag, with multi-pointed antlers, proudly erect on a mountain spur; a waterfall shimmering in sunlight dropping into an endless, wooded valley; wind-teased clouds.

There was no reason for it that he could think of, unless it was the racing clouds; unless it was – was what? – the confidence of an animal in what appeared to be a dangerous situation; unless –

'I bet anything, he's not cursing the wind,' the boy said. 'He's probably thinking how lucky he is to have a decent safety belt. Or how good it's going to be when he comes down.' The boy laughed at his own one-sided conversation.

The man, engrossed with his task, had not seen the cyclist beneath him, he didn't see him turn and ride back the way he had come. He was unconscious of the extent of his influence on a country kid, of the burgeoning of answers to troublesome questions in the mind of a boy, reared in a sheltered valley. Questions the boy could not take back to the valley for answers.

Bern turned right in to Marine Terrace with the wind behind him. He coasted down the hill to the wharf gates. He stopped to watch a team of four horses drawing a wagon, loaded high with potatoes, cross the road in front of him. The potatoes came from where he had come. They would be going to Sydney.

The driver raised his whip and nodded a greeting to the boy on a bike. The boy noticed the driver's face and clothes were covered with dust he had picked up on the journey.

MOORLEAH DANCE

He would go to the dance at Moorleah!

Why not?

It had been vaguely in his mind for – probably for weeks. It was when he was washing off the worst of the dirt before his shower that he made the decision.

All afternoon he had been helping his father renew a culvert where they crossed the creek on to the Far Flat. There was only the one cow to milk, (the others had been dried off, thank goodness). He almost dreaded when they would be coming in again. New calves to teach how to drink, mud, cold rain, pigs, cattle, potatoes to pick over (soon to plant again), repair fences, ferns to cut –

'Do you want to milk Pansy?'

'No. You go, Dad. I'll finish off here.'

His father had looked at what there was to do: nothing much. 'Well don't be long. You go and have a clean-up. It's late enough.'

The boy had purposefully splashed his face with the black mud, shovelling out that last bit from the drain. It would look as if he had been really working, or something. He could have washed off all the worst of it, the black ash from the old shell they had used for the crossing, and the black mud which came off easily when it was wet, washed it in the drain, gone home looking relatively clean (as if he hadn't done much at all).

'Oh dear, you poor old thing. You *have* been working. I'll get you some warm water and soap to take the worst of it off before you shower.'

'And here's some warm black currant – from our own bushes.'

Just a wee feeling of guilt. Damn it, it wasn't Mum or home he was sick of, or the farm so much. But work; bloody; bloody work. To think how he had skited to his school friends about going on the farm. 'Gee, you're lucky!' And he really thought he was, at the time.

'Wouldn't you like to have Donald or someone out for a few days?'

'Wouldn't you like to ride over to Burnie to stay with Donald for the weekend? I'm sure he'd like to see you. And I know Mrs McCabe said –'

But he didn't want to. He didn't want to admit what his parents both thought was a little heaven was – wasn't what he had expected, what he had hoped, no, believed.

He didn't see much of the locals either. Jack went to an occasional dance at Moorleah, not that he danced much, if at all, but it was something. There were girls there. The only girls he ever met now were Judy's friends, who were a few years older and still regarded him as 'a kid'. 'You ought to go sometime,' Jack had said. 'There's one there next Saturday.' 'Yes, I will, sometime.'

But he had missed that one, and the next. It took courage for a kid to burst out into a man's world.

'I think I'll go to the dance tonight, Mum.' Did he sound casual?

'Oh!' She was obviously surprised, but recovered quickly. 'Where is it? The dance.'

'Moorleah.'

'How will you go?'

'Walk.'

'It's a long way.'

'Only about two miles, across the paddocks.' Night time, strange country, strange everything. Don't worry, Mumma!

'Yee-es.' And smiled. 'All right, dear. I'll look out something for you to wear.'

He'd been home on the farm for what seemed like – well it was only about six months, he realized. Frank was working with Graham on a sheep station at Cobar, Loch on his uncle's farm in New Zealand, Judy, nursing at the Mersey Hospital (the same her grandfather had founded fifty years before), Hong, training to be an officer at the Flinders Naval Base (special intake – bright boy, Henry!) Bern, stuck at home on the farm – what he had always wanted to do. Once!

Lyndon French working there too, during the week. About the same age Lyndon, but bigger, stronger, more able to do the hard work.

Perhaps *he* was the trouble. When he was at school, home was the place to repair to. Home was security, and peace, and pleasure. Now he was home, he *needed* something more. He felt his parents gauging his moods. He knew he was being difficult; he knew he wasn't trying not to be. When letters came from members of the family he was equally as excited as his mother and father. For a short while he was living their lives with them; they would turn up the places in the atlas. Frank and Graham had gone to a party in Nyngan. 'Goodness gracious,' his mother had said, 'Nyngan would be a hundred miles from Buckwaroon.' Dear Frank, I went to a dance at Moorleah! Dear Loch, fancy going all the way to Gisborne for a picnic; and meeting all those lovely people; we have the picture of you and your girl friend on the mantelpiece; she looks lovely! I saw – who did I see? – nobody! Dear Hong, Melbourne seems to be an exciting place; things to see, and do – I've been to see George Arliss in 'Disraeli' (the only time I've been anywhere this year) Dear Jude . . . no need to write to Judy. She kept coming back home when she could. Thank goodness! Judy knew how he felt. Sometimes they had long talks about people and things, boys she had met, people who had come into hospital, nurses' parties, things she had done it might be better if Mum and Dad didn't know about – but she would go again. And no letters would come for a while; and he would be left with his thoughts, and the daily grind of work.

'Have a nice time,' his mother said. 'Do you think you should take a lantern?' 'Would it be better if you took your bike around the road? I know it's longer, but – '

'No, I'll be right. It'll be just as quick across the paddocks.' He had been wondering if he would take the bike; probably would have, if his mother hadn't suggested taking it; but then he had to prove something, that he wasn't scared (or whatever reason she had for suggesting it).

You never know at night whether there's a bull in a paddock or not. He remembered his dad saying how once at Woodrising he had been going home late at night, cross country, through scrub. In the distance he had heard a bull roaring and was feeling pleased he was not in the same paddock as that bloke, when a second bull from no more than a few yards to one side had answered the first. His dad reckoned it was as if someone had fired a starter's pistol. He took off, sprinting the distance to their orchard fence in record time. Afterwards he had no recollection of crossing a small creek, but knew he had done; there was no other way.

He kept thinking of his dad's story as he crossed into Bramich's out of Cullen's. Walk slowly, don't run, they mostly take no notice of you. That's what you're told! When he was a hundred yards out from the fence he could see a mob of humps, obviously cattle resting. He stopped. The night was starry, no moon yet (a full moon should be up shortly) but light enough to see where he was going. He skirted the mob, ready to sprint for the nearest fence if necessary. He was close enough to hear those occasional huge sighs of contentment that cattle make when resting.

Once a beast stood and stretched. It was silhouetted against the eastern sky, its back a deep hollow, its tail held high, the switch a hanging mop; it was obviously looking at him, he could see the cradle of its horns a yard apart at the tips. One of Brum Bramich's bullocks! His hair, which had been threatening to stand on end, in spite of the Californian Poppy, relaxed.

He laughed (rather giggled) his relief. He should probably go over and hug the great neck, so quiet and placid. He had done just that once before, but in daylight; the one Mr Harold Bramich had pointed out, 'Old Tiger, he won't hurt you, Boy, but watch out for those horns, mind –' But not here, not tonight; not in these clothes, all dolled up for the dance.

It was to be his first ever dance outside school, and the time in the Burnie theatre when he partnered Elisabeth Edwards at the C of E Debutante's Ball.

When he reached the end of the track which he knew would lead him to the Moorleah Hall he could hear the sound of music. Again he stopped. What was he doing, going to a dance on his own? He would hardly know anybody. He would probably be one of the youngest and smallest there. Who would want to dance with him anyway? He toyed with the idea of going straight home. But kept on; the hall and the sound of music growing out of the mist of night.

And the mob of young men standing at the entrance to the hall. Hesitantly, he joined them. A few people nodded a greeting, Jack spoke to him and smiled, but no one seemed at all concerned whether he was there or not. They didn't appear to be even curious. He was accepted, as a fox terrier would be, joining a group of cross-bred cattle-dogs, as of no real account; for which, he supposed, he was grateful in a way, even if a little humiliated.

People kept coming, some walking, some on bikes or motor bikes, and one lot, a rowdy crowd in an A model. It seemed impossible that ten people could come out of it, but they did: five young men and their girl friends; a jumble of legs and laughter as they got on to the gravel; a couple of the girls, as they slid out, even showing their suspenders, until they stood up and shook their dresses down around their shoes.

'Burnie lot! I've seen that red-'eaded bastard before. Always lookin' for trouble. He'll find it 'ere, no worry, if that's what 'e wants.' Bern looked at the speaker. The others had called him Biscuit. He looked as if he could run a mile with a bag of spuds under each arm, and, Bern thought, dumb enough to do just that.

Still chiacking each other, the new arrivals walked over to the hall, taking little notice of the locals who reluctantly made a lane for them to enter, and closed in behind them as they bunched up at the table inside, while they bought their tickets.

Unlike the locals, most of whom left their girlfriend, (if they had one) to pay her own way in and themselves stayed cluttering up the porch and entrance, the visitors sat inside with their girls on the wooden benches which, except for the end where the band was, lined the walls.

Old Peter, the MC, who claimed not to have missed a Moorleah dance for ten years, shouted out above the din of talk and laughter, 'Will the gents please take their partners for a fox-trot!'

Some of the watchers at the doorway butted their smokes, jammed the butt in behind their ears and slouched in to pick a partner ('Do yer wanta dance?') from the girls lined up along the walls like exhibits waiting to be judged. Some men were content to stand (the whole night, Bern realized afterwards) watching who got who and ready to talk with anyone who came out for a breather.

'I see Bluey is goin' fertha red-'eaded sheila from Sisters.'
'Ay! Get a load of old Biscuit, will yer, the way he's swingin'

that left mitt of his he'll clock some bastard, for sure.' 'Why don'yer give that blonde wi' the pink dress a trundle?' If the man the others called Kanga hadn't given him a sharp dig in the ribs with his elbow, Bern wouldn't have known he was talking to *him*. He stretched forwards to look at the girl. She was about his age and small, her face was pinched, but, he thought, quite attractive, her arms, bare to the elbow, were terribly thin. She was sitting next to a woman who could have been her older sister or her mother; her face was so dolled up with powder and paint it was hard to tell her age.

Bern looked up at Kanga's grinning face. 'All right,' he said. 'I'll ask the little blonde, if you go for her mother.'

Kanga's 'Haw, haw!' caused several people dancing near the entrance to look over in their direction. Bern ducked back out of sight, embarrassed.

'Bloody mother! I like that! That's Shirl! Shirl's been the belle of the ball a few times in her day. You gotta know Shirl, don'yer? Haven't yer been 'ere before? Is this yer first dance, like? Ol' Shirl! 'er bloody mother! Haw, haw!'

'Yes,' Bern said, answering the last question first. Kanga was satisfied. Or he seemed to be. But clung a little longer to the notion which apparently intrigued him. 'Me dance with ol' Shirl! Aw, Jeez! Shirl's all right, though. Mightn't get that many dances, like, but comes inter'er own when the dance finishes like, if yer know whatta mean.' And surprises him again with an elbow jab, which makes him grunt a bit.

'Ever seen Kanga hop?' somebody said. It was Tom, happy Tom, good-looking Tom, until he opened his mouth to smile and those teeth: two front ones missing, framed by several with black holes and a skin of yellow scum, which he scratched from time to time with his finger nail, and washed with his tongue, and chewed, as if he were really eating something. 'Jeez, that's how 'e got 'is name. Hopped around like a big roo. The sheilas put a ban on 'im in the finish, for more reasons than one.'

'Jus' when you're ready,' Kanga said. But patiently. You could tell he and Tom were good mates. But Kanga didn't have a chance to say anything more before the one they called Teapot came bursting in to the group. 'Hey,' Teapot said, 'look what I found, over in the Ford. There's a dozen in a box on the floor.'

They were all staring at Teapot who was grinning like an idiot and holding a bottle of Cascade in a hand which looked to be all out of proportion to his size: almost, Bern was thinking, as big as Biscuit's, and his was the biggest hand he had ever seen. Apart from his hands, Teapot wasn't much bigger than Bern. Someone had given him a basin cut, someone who either didn't know or didn't care what sort of a cut he got, horizontal ledges running right around the back of his head, and that straw-coloured mop, looking as if it had been sat there on top and would topple off any minute.

'Let's git into it,' someone said. But Kanga was thinking, 'Wait a bit Teapot. You go over and put it back where you found it.'

'Put it back! Gawd, Kanga, they wouldn't miss a couple.'

'Now listen you blokes. We'll have 'em all right, but we gotta be a bit careful. We don't want no trouble. You're sure they're all Cascade?'

'Yes, it's a new box. They've only had a couple out of it.'

'Right. This dance'll be finished any minute and those blokes'll be out to crack another couple of bottles. Teapot, you and a couple of others go and get a few empties off the heap in the blackberries at the back of the shithouse; good clean ones mind, and they gotta be Boags.'

'There's a tremendous waste of talent,' Bern's mother had said once. 'If only they had the opportunity —' She was talking about the poor, those school children who were forced to work before and after school. He thought a bit about what she had said while Kanga organized the transfer of the beer from the Cascade bottles into the old Boags

162

empties, after the start of the second dance: how he had carefully lifted off the caps with the bottom of his Town Talk tobacco tin, and put them back on the Boags.

'Now put them out'a sight, fer Chrissake!' Referring to the Cascade empties.

Kanga held up a bottle, with the label showing, when the Burnieytes trooped out at the end of the dance. 'Want a drink, mate?' Kanga said, as friendly as could be. And the big red-head stopped and looked at Kanga holding out the bottle. 'Got another couple where they came from,' Kanga said, with his big friendly grin.

'Boags,' the red-head said. 'Better than nothing. Thanks, mate.' He took the bottle, wiped the neck with his hand and gulped down a couple of mouthfuls and handed it on to his friends, while Kanga flipped the top off another. 'Nothin' like sharin' a bit o' grog with yer mates,' Kanga said, handing the bottle on around the circle.

Bern was surprised, but pleased to realize he was a part of the circle. Tom handed him the bottle. He was unsure whether he should wipe the mouth of the bottle or not. And didn't. He took one gulp and felt suddenly a bit sick, that he might be swallowing some of Tom's teeth cleanings. 'Must go for a leak,' he said, thinking that when he came back it wouldn't be next to Tom. And anyway he wanted to miss a round or two because he knew that he'd only need about three drinks and he wouldn't know the way home.

He heard the yell from where he was standing, 'Hey, Red, someone's swiped all our grog. There's not a fuckin' bottle left!'

'Cut that swearing!' It was Biscuit, Bern could tell. 'We don't 'ave swearing 'ere, there could be women around.'

Bern stopped back in the shadows, half excited, half fearful. He had heard about this sort of thing before: 'There was a big shindy out at Sisters last night' or 'You should have seen the free-for-all at the Myalla dance on Saturday night' and his dad would shake his head and say 'Tch – Tch! It's the alcohol.' (He didn't realize at the time that his dad's brother had died an alcoholic aged thirty-five, and his Great Uncle Russell, who had caused the family 'a great deal of anxiety' had been sent to Tasmania with a letter of introduction to Governor Arthur, where he had 'died of apoplexy in the street', in 1834.)

Biscuit had obviously come out for a talk or a smoke. Bern could see him half a head taller than anyone else, and glowering at the man at the car door. He could see Red-head too, looking first at his mate, then at Biscuit, then at the label on the bottle in his hand. One wrong word!

But Kanga had a right one, 'Pinched! Then he wasn't one of youse blokes?'

'Who wasn't?'

'Didn't take that much notice. A bloke pulled up a while back. Old T model – had a woman with him – walked over to the car, large as life, took out a box, took it over to his car, unloaded whatever it was in it, brought back the empty box, said somethin' about "If you see Ned or Red, or some name like that – tell 'im I got the stuff all right".'

'This bloke. What did he look like?'

'He was only a little bloke.' Teapot was jumping up and down in his excitement. 'Had on an old coat and a red sweat-rag around his neck. Didn't he, Kanga?'

'An' dungaree trousers with patches all over 'em,' said Tom.

'An' a big hat with a feather in it.' Biscuit wasn't going to be left out of it.

And Teapot laughed.

Red-head turned on him. 'Youse bastards tryin' to have us on?'

'I thought I said to cut that swearin,' Biscuit said, full of menace, shaking his fist in Red-head's face.

Bern had heard the car coming down past Roy Clark's

place and saw the lights before they did. He saw a jumble of bodies and fists being thrown. Then Teapot yelled, 'Plice. It's Old Mick.'

He was right. As the Baby Austin turned in to pull up beside the A model, they could see the two policemen with their heads nearly poking through the roof.

By the time they were out of the car everybody was standing around peacefully, except Kanga and Tom who had stacked the bottles up under the bench in the porch and were sitting there leaning forwards as if they had been there for an hour. Kanga had just rolled himself a smoke and was handing the tin and the Tally-ho 'tishers' to Tom.

'What's going on here?' Mick said. 'No trouble, I hope.'

'Just a bit of a haltercation, Officer,' Teapot said. 'They reckoned we pinched their grog.' Nodding to Red-head and his mates. 'And we didn't, didn't we, Biscuit. It was someone pulled up in a T model dressed up in a –'

'Shut up, fer Chrissake, Teapot,' Kanga said, sort of to himself.

The policeman looked at Teapot. (He knew all about him; had struck him before. A fool, get himself and everybody else in trouble. One or two in every town. Goodnatured idiots.) He looked from one to the other, not saying anything, noticing the graze on Biscuit's eyebrow. Whoever put that there must be able to handle himself, or else he was plain lucky. He saw there were a few strangers amongst them. (Mick was always a bit suspicious of strangers on his territory; the red-headed one, he had seen at a dance at Somerset a week or two ago, caused a bit of trouble there.)

'What's your name?'

'Red.'

'Red who?'

'Smith.'

'Red Smith. Sure it's not Brown?'

'Smith.'

'Where are you from?'

'Burnie.'

'Long way to come for a dance, Red?'

'Taint that far.'

'Well, it's not that far back again, then, is it?' (No answer.)

'Somebody pinch your grog, did they, Red?'

'We didn't have any grog.'

'Didn't 'ave any!' Teapot exploded. 'They told us they had a whole box of Cascade. An' they reckoned that we pinched it, but we didn't. (As if he had convinced himself.) It was Boags what we –'

'Oh Jeez!' Kanga said, and hung his head as if he were praying.

'Who said we had Cascade?' Red was no fool.

'Enough of that argument,' Mick said. 'I'm not here to bandy words.'

Red was looking hard at Teapot. And Teapot was looking at everybody, one after the other, with a pleased grin on his face. And Mick's off-sider came over from the A model with an empty Cascade box and showed Mick. And Mick looked at Teapot, and decided against. There was something like-able about the silly little bugger and anyway he was a local. 'How did you get a name like that?' he had asked him once. And Teapot had undone the buttons on his strides and pulled out his dick: 'They reckon I got a big spout,' he had said, proud as you like. And doubled up with laughter when someone had added, 'And nothin under his lid but a big black hole.'

Mick turned to Red.

'Red Smith,' he said. 'Take this as an official warning! If ever I catch you again with alcoholic beverages within the precincts of a place of public entertainment, or causing your-self to be a public nuisance in the eyes of the law, you will be charged and brought before the court. Now get to hell back

to where you came from and quick, before I'm forced to kick
your quoit out of it.'

It was a long speech for Constable Kelleher. He was not
given to a lot of talk. Law enforcement was mostly attained
by persuasion, with the boot if necessary.

'You didn't catch me with no alcohol —'

'Listen, Smith. If I say you had alcohol, you had alcohol,
whether you had alcohol or not. Now get moving.'

When the A model had left, skidding up the gravel, and
the dancers had all stopped crowding around the door, and
the music had started again, Mick looked at Kanga and Tom
sitting on the bench. 'You blokes had a hard day,' Mick said.

'Too right! Cuttin' wood. Knocks you around a bit.'

'Yes. Haven't seen you two look so knocked up for a long
time. Anyway we better get going.'

He stopped on the way to the car. 'Tell Teapot not to talk
so much. He might get into trouble.'

Bern watched the tail-light disappear over the hill. Kanga
was opening another bottle.

'Do you reckon he guessed?'

'He didn't guess. He knew,' Kanga said. 'Good luck!' And
upended the bottle.

Bern went into the hall. He felt everyone would be looking at him. He walked straight across to where the blonde
girl and Shirl were still sitting. He stopped in front of the
blonde. 'Excuse me,' he said. 'May I have the pleasure of a
dance?' and bowed slightly as he had been taught.

TALKING WITH VICTOR

Ben sat on the back step with the spaniel's head resting awkwardly against his right leg. He fiddled absently with the dog's floppy ear. Inside, he could hear his younger brother telling his mother how he gives the trainees a hurry along. 'They've got no understanding of discipline.'

He wondered whether he had been sitting on the same step a couple of years ago when Hong had been complaining bitterly about the unfairness, the stupidity of the same treatment that he was now helping to dish out to the new intake. He smiled to himself as he recalled the conversation:

'But it's so stupid,' Hong had said. 'It's quite unreasonable. There's a bell and a time for everything: for getting out of bed, going to breakfast, inspection, parade, everything. If you don't do everything exactly according to the standards as laid down, then you're penalized. I had my weekend leave cancelled simply because my bed was, according to the inspecting officer, not properly made.'

'Goodness, they are strict!'

'Not strict! Stupid! The only way I could be sure of getting everything in order was to get up before the first bell. I didn't mind doing that, and things went well until I was caught out of bed before the bell and warned never to do that again. I just lie there waiting for the bell. It's crazy!'

It was crazy then, and it's still crazy, Bern is thinking. He

168

wonders whether his mother thinks so too. How do you go about indoctrinating people? Was it indoctrination, or was it a normal desire to exact vengeance, like a boy who is belted by his father for no good reason, does he grow up to bash his own children?

Not a question he could be fussed about. Particularly on a day like this. One of those March evenings when, if you shut your eyes, the sounds of birds, and calves bawling, and someone laughing, and the hum of bees still working, seem not to be noises, but concrete images painted on a slide, one you could light up, like on Bill Touzeau's magic lantern.

'What do you think, Vic?' And the dog opened his top eye and winked, and shut it again.

Peace.

Frank still pottering with his bike: the tinkling of a wrench on the garage floor, the phooo – phooo – phooo, as he kicks the starter but good luck, no bark, no shattering, splintering, of the – of the what? – curtain of evening. Hardly curtain – of the what then, Vic? Don't even open the eye. Don't know, don't matter, don't care, you lazy old hound-dog.

Funny, Frank could have been in the bank instead of him, or as well as; he had passed his banker's entrance exam, hadn't he? years ago, but didn't want it. Preferred the open air: cane cutting, traipsing around Queensland, outback New South Wales, moving, moving – fit and (what do they say) fancy-free – now he's settling – for a while – Major Harcourt's six month training course in Hobart for unemployed, over, finished; now a trainee fitter at the Zinc Works – seemed content enough when he stayed with him at Sargeant's in Murray Street. Mr Sargeant, a truck driver, had a heart problem or something, and Frank used to crank his engine for him in the mornings. Nice people – lovely little girl.

Then the phooo – phooo – phooo again, and suddenly it

fires – thromm – thromm – thromm – slow but loud, then blurring as he revs the engine. He's got the exhaust off. A mob of starlings takes off from the elm tree. He's away up the paddock – brrmmm – brrmmm as he changes gears, up, down, up, testing something. He's got an ear for a motor, Frank. (What a pilot he would have made. Silly people!) The AJS a lot more powerful than Loch's little Raleigh. But how about the 5hp Citroen! Sylvia Redwing.

They told him he was got at!

'It looks lovely, dear,' his mother had said, admiring the homemade body painted with silverfrost and the front mud-guards a robin red. 'But seventy pounds; do you think you can afford it?' And his father had looked at the engine, (which to him was a complicated mess of wires and steel which could, he was sure, be quite unpredictable) and said: 'Hmmmm.' And hmmmm, it was, when Bern and two friends he had taken down to Boat Harbour beach had all to get out coming back up the steep hill and push the thing, with the engine full revs, held on with a stick fixed across the accelerator pedal. And hmmmm it was again, when he had driven up to Latrobe to collect Judy for her weekend off, and the gear box had dropped out on the road on the way home.

A disastrous trip that one! They had called at Aunt Mary's house at the ES&A Bank in Devonport. 'Judith! and Bernard! How lovely to see you both. Come and have a cup of tea.' And as they settled in the kitchen, 'How is your work, Judith?'

'Good thankyou, Aunt Mary. I'm working in ID at the moment.'

'Oh, are you. And what is ID?'

'Infectious diseases.'

Hand to her mouth, Aunt Mary's normally rosy cheeks visibly blanching. 'Oh dear, I forgot. Whatever is the time? I'm supposed to be – I had completely forgotten – you must call again sometime.' And all the time being hustled down the passage and out on to the street.

So, he had found himself riding his push-bike to Wynyard on Monday mornings and boarding at Richardson's during the week. After all the car was really a luxury. Loch managed on the farm with his Raleigh and the occasional trip in the Rugby.

Bern watched his older brother wheel another (must be the third) wheelbarrow load of cowdung and leaf mould into the garden. Such industry and order! He certainly intended to leave behind a perfect garden!

When Loch was in New Zealand, Bern had tried to keep up the vegie garden but it had never looked like this. That was a few years ago now. His mother had written: *Loch dear, would you mind coming back on to the farm? Bern has found it a bit hard and has applied and been accepted for a job with the Bank of Australasia in Burnie, to start in January.*

Of course, Loch had come home – of course because he was, always had been, the backstop, the reliable worker, content to remain at home, content to do whatever was required, and more. The vegetable garden his after-hours job; one which he guarded jealously.

A fitness fanatic – on top of a long day's work, he religiously did his nightly exercises, his one thousand skips, his deep breathing, drank his glass of water (it must be well water, because of the mineral content) and thumped his solar plexus with both fists swinging alternately wham, wham, wham. 'Here Scrub, (or Tom as he affectionately called his younger brother), hit me here. Harder! And again!' Until the bulging muscle, flexed, was hard as iron.

Cricket and swimming his loves. 'Who is that?' People on the beach at Boat Harbour would point at the dot on the water and the two arms, one-two, one-two, one-two, that never faltered, perfect rhythm. 'I dunno' or maybe 'Loch Roberts', if they knew. 'What's he doing?' 'Swimming.' 'I can see that. What's he out there for. The sharks'll get him.'

'They won't get him!' And they never did, of course.

And his cricket! Bill O'Reilly and Clarrie Grimmet his heroes, and Bradman, but he didn't pretend to be a batsman. He'd talk us into standing behind the wickets, no batsman, stop the ball and throw it back; move the disc where he had to land the ball; leg side, off side, straight on; leg break, off break, wrong'un. Oh well, it was his way, and it seemed to work all right. 'What d'you reckon, Vic? You're his dog. You should know.' And the brown eye opened. In fact he lifted his head and looked down the garden, then satisfied all was in order, flopped his heavy head back against Bern's leg.

But probably he wasn't looking at Loch at all. He had heard Judy and her father coming up from putting the calves in another paddock. His dad didn't top the yearling sales most years at the Wynyard Show Sales for nothing. When they're weaned off new milk, give them a slug of mutton bird oil each, once a day, (and take a mouthful himself) straight from the bottle. Ugh! Put them on clean fresh grass every week or two, remember what Confucius say: farmer's best manure is farmer's footsteps.

They were laughing about something. Judy was wearing a pair of Frank's work trousers and a khaki shirt. With her hair tied back in a scarf she looked boyish and athletic. Her father was twirling a coil of rope, which flashed his mind back, how many, at least twelve years: the Boat Harbour School picnic-sports at the beach; Kay Roberts and Norm Dobson holding the rope and Judy and Lilla Dobson ran a dead heat. Because he and Hong were proud of their big sister they had joined in the chant. Roberts and Dobson holding the rope, Roberts and Dobson won. At the time it was a big thing; all these years later it seemed such a piddling thing to remember. He decided that what was significant today would be regarded as trivial some time in the future and vice versa. Like his foot. Vic, that great, bony head of yours – eeeease over – that's it. Don't even open that eye,

172

will you, Mongrel?

Like his and Judy's love affairs. His as good as over. Sad! Nice girl, Peg. Warm, cuddly. Probably happy with someone else. How's your love-life, Jude? She'd smile today. Ever since she came home, she's been happy with everybody, as if they're making her happy, an' it's nothing t'do with that. All because of some Algie bloke. Who is Algie? Algie who? You all prick up your ears. Is it an old family name? – a name you can just let drop, like: Jude is friendly with one of the you-know-whos. But she pretends to be casual. Just someone I met, she says. You can always tell: things going along all right, and everything is sweet; big break or disappointment, and prickly as hell – at first you wonder what you've done wrong.

Good to see her happy though, Ju-ju-chocolate-lolly. They don't call her that now. The only reason they ever did, it was a sure way of making her mad.

Good to see everybody happy. God knows where we'll all be next year, our tight little family. But good to feel happy, eh, Vic? Aaarrr. 'Sthat all you can say, ol' friend? Turn that great, floppy ear of yours inside out – thought as much, a blackberry thorn – there – and you didn't even flinch.

Hong and his mother are laughing about some prank he'd been up to at Flinders. He seems to be happy enough there now. Seems everybody is for once. Perhaps it's because it's the first time for a couple of years they've all been together at home.

Even Bern is happy, which is something. He wonders about what control anybody has over their life: the ups and downs, the good days, the bad days, accidents that happen, sicknesses, luck, even the weather. Like throwing a bottle into the middle of Bass Strait: maybe it will sail on for ever, maybe splinter on a rock the first day, bring little fish to wonder for a while what those shafts of light are glinting down there.

173

He was getting used to the tossing of the sea; (metaphorically speaking, that is) sometimes riding on the crest of a wave, sometimes deep in the trough. But, oooh Mother, how he hated those first few weeks, or months was it? Roberts, what's this! Roberts, post these cheques! Roberts, close the door! Roberts open the door. Roberts make up Mr Clark's passbook! Now! Never once, a please, never a Christian name, or a 'could you?' – snap! snap! snap! Roberts, take this draft around to Mr Morgan and get enough cash to cover it or, (he knows), it'll be dishonoured, NSF – Not Sufficient Funds.

Ah, that was the worst – Mr Morgan's son a school friend, and this big strong man with a little shop, would see this bank kid coming, who'd see the concern, (never anger) and guilt, and his hands would fiddle through the till and the drawer and back to the till and each time he'd say: 'A bit, er, short at the moment. Er, I'll have it in by, er, three o'clock, tell Mr –'

And the bank kid would go to walk out. He couldn't say 'sorry', or 'that's all right, Mr Morgan', or 'don't worry', or smile. He just wanted to yell out to the world: 'Get off his back! leave him alone!', but that was cranky, that wasn't business, so he'd turn and say, 'Oh, Mr Morgan, I nearly forgot, could I have a packet of State Express, oh, an' a threepenny bar of Cadbury's Energy, please?' He wished he could buy more but how could he, his fortnightly cheque was two pounds fourteen and twopence, and two pounds of that went to Mrs Porte for board and the rest to cover clothes and ceteras (like the pictures once a week, the Old Darwinians dance, a few beers with Aidan, or the boys).

So it went, until one month Mr Morgan didn't make it by three o'clock and the draft was dishonoured NSF, and F. O. Henry wouldn't supply any more stock, and suddenly there was another owner of the shop and the bank kid couldn't bear to go there any more.

But life wasn't all that bad. There were the exchanges when all the juniors from the various banks gathered at a back room of the Union Bank to exchange cheques.

'What's your name?' they'd said, that first time. 'Bernard Roberts.' 'I know that. What are you called?' 'Scrub. But I don't like it much. Don't like Bern either, much.' 'Weeell,' Tim Morris said. 'He works for the Australasia – Asia.' 'Ayrshire,' said another. 'Ayrshire Bull.' 'Scrub Bull.' 'Bull Roberts.' 'Welcome to the Exchanges, Bull!'

The exchanges; to exchange news and gossip as well as cheques: Snow Lewis, breaking his own Wynyard to Burnie speed record; and one day a train had whistled as he sped around the corner into Somerset, and a team of horses had taken fright and closed off the road, and Snow, with no road left, had taken to the paddocks. 'You lucky bastard, Lewis, to limp in an hour late, with only a crashed bike.'

And smutty jokes, and nasty tales of nasty senior officers: how for instance the teller at the Commercial was not given time off and warned that if he went to a bank officer's union meeting he could face dismissal. But he had gone and the union had threatened to strike if any officer were sacked, and nobody was, and a few weeks later everyone got a pay-rise.

There was the manager, Mr George Sorell, who also called him Roberts, but in a different and friendly way. Several times Roberts had to sleep at the bank when Mr Sorell went away. The thing was that a bank officer must at all times sleep on the premises to protect the bank's property, to guard against thieves. It happened that this very junior employee was asked very nicely by the manager to sleep in a small guest room upstairs for two nights while Mr and Mrs Sorell went to Great Lake for two nights.

'We shall be back late on Sunday, Roberts,' Mr Sorell said after showing him his room. 'Now there is one other thing. You will need to keep a loaded revolver at your bedside. Have you ever used one of these?'

It was nothing like the little silver .22 of Frank's. He could handle that one all right. Bang! bang! bang! Take it down to the beach, somewhere quiet, do what Frank does, throw a tin in the air and hit it twice before it touches ground. This one looked much the same as the heavy and cumbersome .45 that his father kept underneath the sheets at the back of the white cupboard in the boy's room. Much the same as the one that a young man had shown him on his way home from high school years before.

He had caught up with this man on a pushbike on a lonely stretch of road near Mackenzie's. 'Have you ever used one of these?' the man had said, suddenly flashing the revolver. 'No.' (With bristles rising, skin prickling.) Then he would show him. Put a stone on the post and, 'Hold your right wrist with your left hand, extend it full stretch like this, and pull the trigger.' All of which he did. And the thing bucked so much he felt the bullet almost might have put a hole through the peak of his green school cap. (Perhaps he would have hit the tin if someone had thrown it up.)

So Roberts said in reply to Mr Sorell, 'Yes, sir. Once, sir.' To which Mr Sorell said, 'Good.' And shook out a handful of bullets into a small box. 'I'll leave these on your bedside table.' Which is where Roberts found them when late on the Friday evening he cautiously let himself into the spooky kitchen and climbed silently upstairs. He turned on the light and sure enough there was the revolver. Hurriedly he filled the chamber with bullets, which gave him a strange feeling of security. He shut his door, pointed the revolver at the door knob, held his wrist, then aimed about a foot low. He wondered where the bullet would go if he were to pull the trigger.

He undressed, turned out the light, and stood looking out the window at the bit of Cattley Street he could see, and the patch of ocean visible below Round Hill, dancing in moonlight. A light went on in an upstairs room of the Launceston

Bank for Savings opposite. He watched Sibyl Emmett, the bank manager's daughter, (who had been in his class at school, and had been a well developed girl in those days, two years before) getting undressed ready for bed.

'My name is Aeneas,' the young bank officer whispered. 'Please, O Prophetess, lead me to the Underworld.' And for as long as it took, the dreaded thought of a bank robber left his mind.

But on the second night at approximately two a.m., Roberts was awakened by what sounded like a creaking stair, followed soon by the unmistakable sound of footsteps passing softly along the passage. He put his skinny arm out and gained confidence through the feel of the revolver. After a time he slipped out of bed, with the revolver in hand, he slowly eased open the door and stood in the passage. Around the corner he could see a glimmer of light which could have been moonlight showing through a window.

He sneaked down the passage, turned the corner and continued until he could see indistinctly, but definitely, the toes of a pair of boots just inside a room. Someone was there!

He grabbed his right wrist, held the revolver up, to aim waist high, and almost shouted, 'Come out!' to which Mr Sorell replied sleepily. 'Is that you, Roberts?'

'Er – yes, sir,'

'We decided to come home. The weather was terrible. We tried not to wake you.'

'That's all right, sir. Goodnight, sir.'

'Goodnight, Roberts. See you in the morning. Not too early.'

'Yes, sir. No, sir. Goodnight, sir.'

O yes, Vic, old son, there were the ups and downs all right – just let him shift that leg a bit – strange how content dogs apppear to be to lie for ever, and how they like to feel contact with a person.

There's Loch off again whistling 'Love Letters in the Sand'.

He'll be on to 'K-k-k-katie' next, or 'Home on the Range'. Tomorrow's Sunday, probably hear him go through the hymns: 'Rock of Ages', 'Lead Kindly Light', 'There Were Ninety and Nine' – all those old ones, when he's cleaning up the cowshed (that's if he is – perhaps someone should offer) a voice that carries. From the house, you could hear everything he said in the cowshed when he was talking to his dad. You knew his dad had answered by what Loch said – a one-sided conversation – there's a game: fill in the other voice!

Bridge, five hundred, pontoon, poker – oh yes, and crib with the gang at Park House: Peter and Guy and Bern (three exchange boys) and Max Green with 7BU (a stepping stone to bigger things for Max) nice bloke, soft spoken, artist's model type, inhaled his cig smoke twice, second time curled gracefully up his nose, anyone else try they'd be sure to have one blocked nostril, and look crude; not Max.

There were good times. Outside work, that is. Exciting, Bern found it. A life his mother and father didn't know about, wouldn't understand. There was so much he couldn't discuss with them. Everything had changed since they were young – not just wireless, telephone and light – people's attitudes and philosophies were different, more broad-minded. In a way he felt he had to protect his parents from this new world his generation had discovered.

For years, they, particularly his father, had become obsessed about world affairs. At first it had been the war in Spain. His father reorganized his meal times to coincide with 'The News' and 'Notes on the News'. Why? He wondered. It all depressed him so. He would sigh and shake his head and remain silent for so long. 'That Franco! There is something diabolical about the man and his connection with the Pope. To think the Church could offer support for such heathenish and barbarous behaviour!'

Then the bit in the newspaper which he cut out and read sometimes to people who would listen.

'This Goebbels – Doctor of what, I wonder! Listen to this:

Some people say there is a world conscience, which is the League of Nations, whose part it is to preserve world peace, but I prefer to rely on guns. We are beggars. We have no colonies, and no raw materials. We are confronted with problems which cannot be overcome by internal methods. Others have no need for the colonies they have taken from us. It is dangerous for the world to concede to such demands, because someday the bomb will explode.

He who takes up the sword will perish by the sword!'
But now!

Judy and her father are talking about something. Not politics! They are standing there by the ivy stump, looking down towards the willow flat. Maybe memories, Jude is pointing, long arm outstretched. Lots of memories down there, girl! The present is coming down the Lagoon paddock now. You can hear the motor rev, change back for the red hill, through the red gate (which is the bottom one). The two turn to watch as the bike comes barking closer. Vic raises his head. He knows the sound and drops back into sleep. The bike noise stops and Frank is straddling the machine, sitting back, arms folded. Now they're all laughing.

And Hong and his mother inside, still talking; giggle and chatter and the clink of dishes. It's getting late-ish but nobody in a hurry, no one is going anywhere, not tonight: a soft, warm, Tasmanian-March, with night, drifting in, like a yellow leaf settling on water. The sort of evening when Bern and Peg sat on the sand at the North Terrace beach; people coming and going, or huddled in groups, or swimming. Peter Sadler came with his girlfriend. They brought pies and beer. There was no music, no noise much, except people talking, kids playing, feet squeaking in loose sand.

A magic they wanted to hold on to. And did. The full moon came lifting up out of the sea, spilling a yellow glob of light that slid like oil and laid a path directly to them, for

179

their eyes to follow. For a while they watched and said nothing much; desultory talk. They lay back on the sand and his arm ached with the weight of her sweet head resting.

> Whilst yet the calm hours creep
> Dream thou – and from thy sleep
> Then wake to weep.

But all was not lost.

Roberts was transferred to the Wynyard branch. Fairbairn, and Griffiths, both good bosses! Guy Fogg, the teller, a friend in need, a friend in deed. So work not so much a drudgery.

Perhaps Roberts was easier to get along with, Vic! Or knew more.

They fared him well at the Exchanges: Geoff Marshall – Guy Drake – Peter Sadler – Snow Lewis – Fred Humffray, with their unsung bitty ditty which went with a Barling briar (much, much too expensive for a junior clerk to buy).

> To Scrub Bull Roberts, our public nuisance
> We make this little gift
> Tho' oft that grinning dial of his
> We'd dearly like to lift.
> Empty pockets now we have
> By granting our little whim.
> We all join in the chorus though
> 'Tis worth it to get rid of him.

Get rid of him, they did, Vic boy. To twelve whole miles away. To work in a quiet town; to rowing up the Inglis to the bridge and drifting back on the current, with feet spread-eagled, resting on the rowlocks, playing the mouth-organ to silver gulls on anchored fishing boats rocking to the slap of wavelets on their bows; and gums and wattles, silent watchers.

Moments to store for future use, for God knows when and where. Or why.

Except there is a war on.

Did they tell you there is a war on, Dog? That the glum

and dreary prospect of a bank clerk's life is finished? That men are wanted, Hound, as volunteers, to fight for His Majesty the King (one of the Georges, isn't it?) all food and clothing found, free board and lodging, travel paid to lands beyond the baths of all the western stars. It may be they shall touch the Happy Isles. They don't think too much about the may-bes.

They'll miss you, you great liver and white spaniel, and you'll miss them. Yes them. They'll all be going off somewhere. Hong, the up and coming admiral. Frank, a restless soul, God knows! He's tried twice to join the airforce. And they rejected him on account of his psoriasis. What idiots! Loch and Bern – they both spent time in the 12/50th militia, got used to the rough and tumble – both of them have joined the A.I.F., Vic. And Jude – there ain't no nursing jobs 'round here, old mate.

They made some pretty speeches at the Flowerdale school last night: these boys who've heard the call – true Anzac tradition – unselfishness. Makes you wonder who's fooling who. Perhaps that's what life is all about.

Do you know they tried to teach them how to shoot? Dick Andrews, First World War instructor, lined them up on their bellies, he, on his, looking up the spout of each barrel in turn, checking the position of arms, hands, head, 'Shut your left eye, Private Roberts.' (You've got a title in the army) 'What for, Serge?' 'For two reasons: one, because I said so; two, because you can't shoot with two eyes open.' 'I've always shot with two eyes open, Serge!' 'Then, because I said so.' 'Yes, Serge.'

'See those Germans there?' Serge says. 'They're not bags of straw; they're bloody Germans. And you blokes have got to get 'em! Right?' 'Fix bayonets! Charge! Right breast! Left breast! Neck! Stomach! Groin! In – out! In – out! In – out!'

Old Feathertop! Remember Feathertop, Vic? Nathaniel Hawthorne's story, scarecrow turned into a gentleman?

Course you don't. Didn't do English, did you, mate?

It's all a fake! But only dogs and children see the truth. They are not children any longer, Vic, these soldiers. Or else they'd know those Germans hanging there were really bags of straw.